WITHDRAWN
THE RECORDS OF THE
NENT PUBLIC LIBRARY

D1153674

SPECIAL MESSAGE TO READERS

This book is published under the auspices of

THE ULVERSCROFT FOUNDATION

(registered charity No. 264873 UK)

Established in 1972 to provide funds for research, diagnosis and treatment of eye diseases.

Examples of contributions made are: —

A Children's Assessment Unit at Moorfield's Hospital, London.

•

Twin operating theatres at the Western Ophthalmic Hospital, London.

•

A Chair of Ophthalmology at the Royal Australian College of Ophthalmologists.

•

The Ulverscroft Children's Eye Unit at the Great Ormond Street Hospital For Sick Children, London.

You can help further the work of the Foundation by making a donation or leaving a legacy. Every contribution, no matter how small, is received with gratitude. Please write for details to:

THE ULVERSCROFT FOUNDATION,
The Green, Bradgate Road, Anstey,
Leicester LE7 7FU, England.
Telephone: (0116) 236 4325

In Australia write to:

THE ULVERSCROFT FOUNDATION,
c/o The Royal Australian and New Zealand
College of Ophthalmologists,
94-98, Chalmers Street, Surry Hills,
N.S.W. 2010, Australia

THE CRIMSON RAMBLER

The murder at Darnworth Manor was particularly baffling. Autocratic financier Warner Darnworth had been working alone in his study. The study door was locked on the inside, and the only window was of the non-opening variety. Yet Darnworth had been found slumped over his desk, shot through the head. No weapon was found, either in the room or anywhere else in the manor. To add to the problems of Chief Inspector Gossage and Sergeant Blair, every member of Darnworth's family had good reason to hate him.

Books by John Russell Fearn
in the Linford Mystery Library:

THE TATTOO MURDERS
VISION SINISTER
THE SILVERED CAGE
WITHIN THAT ROOM!
REFLECTED GLORY

JOHN RUSSELL FEARN

THE CRIMSON RAMBLER

Complete and Unabridged

LINFORD
Leicester

First published in Great Britain

First Linford Edition
published 2006

British Library CIP Data

Fearn, John Russell, *1908 – 1960*
The crimson rambler.—Large print ed.—
Linford mystery library
1. Detective and mystery stories
2. Large type books
I. Title
823.9′12 [F]

ISBN 1–84617–150–4

Published by
F. A. Thorpe (Publishing)
Anstey, Leicestershire

Set by Words & Graphics Ltd.
Anstey, Leicestershire
Printed and bound in Great Britain by
T. J. International Ltd., Padstow, Cornwall

This book is printed on acid-free paper

1

Hauling 250 pounds of flesh up the staircase leading to the office of Chief Inspector Douglas Gossage at Scotland Yard was not Divisional Inspector Craddock's idea of fun. Sergeant Blair, the chief inspector's right-hand man, opened the office door. His big, square-jawed face with the close-cropped black moustache broke into a grin of welcome.

'Good morning, sir. Been expecting you.'

Craddock was at his most grumpy as he entered the dingy office. It struck him that the place seemed even more cheerless than usual. November gloom outside with a persistent drizzle, grimy weather-smeared windows, a solitary though powerful electric light casting on steel filing cabinets, a big desk, and Sergeant Blair's table and typewriter in the corner.

'Saturday, November 2nd, 1946. The

glamour of Scotland Yard!' Craddock summed up, and took off his hat. ''Morning, sir,' he added formally, moving across the office so that he stood beside the big desk

'Liver, Craddock, or don't you like working on Saturday mornings?'

The man at the desk asked the question as he laid aside his pen. He smiled, too — an immense smile that was half complacent and half amused.

'No, sir, liver's all right. Just those infernal stairs and this dump you work in.'

'If you don't like it you shouldn't get yourself mixed up in murders so complicated that they necessitate you coming here,' Chief Inspector Gossage commented.

The divisional inspector sat down near the desk. What could be seen of Chief Inspector Gossage on the other side of it was very broad and tweed-suited, a tendency toward the prosaic being relieved by a savagely green tie. It was in contrast to the chief inspector's brick-red complexion, an efflorescence which wandered unchecked far beyond the normal confines to the roots of his close-cropped gray hair and the back of his neck. World travel and years in the tropics had completely pickled his fair skin: nor had long walks outdoors, both at his work and for pleasure, softened it any, either . . . The wit at the Yard who had christened him 'The Crimson Rambler' was still anonymous, but whomever he was the phrase was deadly accurate.

'Well how's the grass down in Godalming?' the chief inspector inquired presently, contemplating Craddock with bright blue eyes.

'The grass?' Craddock could take things very literally sometimes. 'I didn't come this far — or this high up — to talk about the grass, sir. It's this business at Darnworth Manor. Murder — sure as eggs. But I just don't see how old Darnworth could have been murdered. It doesn't make sense whichever way you look at it.'

'He died in his study between 7 and 8 o'clock last evening and nobody did it, eh?' Gossage took off his glasses and peered at the paper he had just picked up.

'No weapon was found and everybody has been accounted for. Study door locked on the inside, and the window was one of the sort you can't tamper with — yet the old man got shot in the back of the head!' Gossage clipped his pince-nez back on his nose. 'All right, suppose you try enlarging on your official statement.'

Craddock hunched forward. 'Darnworth Manor is a big, rambling place some hundreds of years old and recently brought up to date. It's 10 miles from Godalming and two and a half from Bexley, the nearest village. The next neighbor to the Darnworths is just outside the village — a veterinary surgeon by the name of Findley.'

Gossage dragged a pipe with an overlong stem from his pocket and began to fill the bowl with tobacco.

'Inspector Hoyle of the local force sent for me,' Craddock went on. 'That was at 8.30. I arrived at the Manor at 8.45, taking with me the divisional surgeon, fingerprint boys, and a photographer. We found Warner Darnworth in the study, shot dead.'

'Who let you in?'

'Mrs. Darnworth.'

'She had a second key, then?'

'No. There's only one key. She had the butler wriggle it out on to a piece of newspaper under the door on the other side. You know the trick. Then it was simple to open the door.'

'Which means we've only Mrs. Darnworth's word for it that the door was locked?'

'And the butler's. And other members of the family, too, because they were present when the key-wriggling was done. No doubt of it that the study door was locked on the inside. It was when the old man didn't come out of his study to dinner at 8 — and all the bangings on the study door couldn't make him respond — that Mrs. Darnworth had the key wriggled out. They found Darnworth shot and sent for the police.'

Gossage passed a thick, freckled hand over his convict haircut and said nothing.

Craddock went on: 'I searched the study, of course, when the boys had been over it for prints, and I had the house searched inside and out. No sign of a weapon anywhere. No trace of footprints in the garden, either. As for a weapon, I went on the assumption that it was a rifle. The doctor said it was a rifle shot as far as he could tell, but the details — the type of weapon, direction of fire, and so on, he couldn't give until after the postmortem. I told him to send the report on to you. Only points we could get were that Darnworth had not been shot from close at hand — and that he had been dead approximately an hour and a quarter. That is, he died about 7.30.'

'Go on,' Gossage invited.

'I questioned everyone in the house . . .'

'Their stories being . . . ?' Gossage picked up four sheets of paper neatly typed that morning by Sergt. Blair. He took off his glasses to read them.

'First, Mrs. Jessica Darnworth, wife of Warner Darnworth, was in her bedroom being dressed by the companion-help, one Louise. Right?'

'Right,' Craddock confirmed. 'But she's out of the running, sir. She's an invalid

— a paralytic — and has been for five years.'

'I see. And Louise?'

'Wishy-washy and faded. Fortyish. Thin-nosed type and avoids conversation.'

Gossage put one of the papers back on the desk.

'Sheila Darnworth, the younger daughter, was playing the piano. Elaine Darnworth, the elder daughter, was not at home the time of her father's death. Neither was Gregory Bride, her fiancé, staying there for the weekend. Sheila's fiancé, Barry Crespin, was fast asleep in his bedroom at the time of the murder. Then there is Preston, the handyman-chauffeur . . . To say nothing of the servants! That is the sum total of house residents and visitors?'

Craddock nodded and Gossage put the papers down.

The chief inspector said: 'Here's the divisional surgeon's report, which you asked him to send on to me.' He handed it across and the divisional inspector read: 'Post-mortem report, (Warner Darnworth deceased): Death caused by entry of a pellet from an air rifle which pierced the skull bone and lodged in the occipital lobe. Death would be instantaneous. The shot, judging from the line of traverse through the skull, came diagonally from above. Pellet (extracted) of the waisted variety and has been handed to Firearms for examination.'

'Air rifle!' Craddock exclaimed. 'That never occurred to me!'

Gossage tossed over another report. 'Take a look at this.'

'Firearms report on pellet presented for inspection (Warner Durnworth deceased): This is a 16-grain pellet from, very probably, the muzzle of a B.S.A. air rifle, which has a muzzle velocity of 600 feet per second. As such, easily capable of penetrating a skull bone at short range.'

'More interesting still,' Craddock commented. What else have we, sir?'

'Report from 'Dabs',' Gossage said, studying it. 'Only fingerprints worth mentioning seem to be those of the dead man. There are others, but they probably belong to the servants.'

He put the fingerprint report down then hunched himself over three enlarged photographs of the dead man's study. The first showed a white-haired man in a silk dressing gown seated in big swivel chair before the desk. He had not slumped across the desk, though his head had dropped forward until his chin touched his breast. His hands were still on the blotter, the fingers clenched and casting shadows on the blotter from the glow of the still lighted, downwardly turned desk light on his right.

The second photograph showed the study in general. On the extreme left was the only door. Diagonal to it was a heavy bureau. Next, in left to right progression, came the floor-to-ceiling shelves lined with books, and the curtained window.

Between the door and the commencement of the shelves, nearly on a line with the heavy Jacobean bookcase on the opposite side of the room, hung a twin-globed electrolier. At the far end of the room, and at the farthest point from the study door, near the window, was the desk at which the dead man was seated.

Other appointments included two leather easy chairs, some ordinary hard-backed chairs, and a table in a corner. The only signs of heating were in the steam pipes before a built-up fireplace.

The third photograph was an enlargement of the wound in the back of the man's head, a wound that had slightly stained the white hair.

The Crimson Rambler clipped the pince-nez back on his nose.

'Now, these folks in the house. Mrs. Jessica Darnworth. An incurable paralytic?'

'That's her story and it seems to be true. We can check on the medical evidence if necessary. She has a wheel-chair. I found her a particularly acid piece of work. About 58. I didn't delve much into the cause of her invalidism. She says that she was in her bedroom until 10 minutes to 8, and had been since 6 o'clock. Then she came downstairs — '

'How? In a wheelchair?'

'That,' Craddock said, 'is where Preston comes in. The chauffeur-handyman. It's part of his job to carry Mrs.

Darnworth about, from wheelchair to bedroom, from wheelchair to car, and so on. He's a taciturn, thin-faced customer with an irritating habit of running his words into one another. Probably wouldn't stop at murder if he could make capital out of it.'

'And what's his story?'

'He was in the main corridor in which Mrs. Darnworth's bedroom is situated, between 7 o'clock and 10 to 8, and he never moved from there. He was waiting for Mrs. Darnworth to call him. Apparently he always does that from 7 to 8 each evening. At any time in that hour she might call him to take her downstairs. It was 10 to 8 when she did call him and he carried her to the wheelchair in the hall.'

'And Louise? How does she fit in?'

'She stayed behind for a moment or two after Mrs. Darnworth had been carried downstairs; then she followed.'

'And Sheila played the piano and Elaine was out?' Gossage added. 'This chap, Gregory Bride — why was he over for the week-end?'

'He's Elaine Darnworth's fiancé, and

he's a scientific inventor. He lives in Godalming, has a house there, but he comes over to the manor a good many weekends. He arrived in his car at 4.30 yesterday afternoon. I understand he came over this weekend to see if old man Darnworth would finance some invention or other. Darnworth did a lot of that sort of thing.'

'And what kind of a fellow is Bride?'

'So-so.' Craddock raised and lowered heavy shoulders. 'A bit stuffy. Very scientific, and high in the collar. He and Elaine Darnworth would make a bonny pair, I'd say. Both highbrow and standoff-ish.'

'There's this other chap — Barry Crespin. He, too, was over for the weekend. Any particular reason?'

'He's been coming every weekend for six months. He's engaged to Sheila, the younger daughter. Not a bad sort of chap. Radio engineer and has a flat in the city.'

'What was he doing in bed at 7.30 in the evening? Was he ill?'

'No. The night before he had been repairing a radio. It took him until early in the morning to locate the fault and correct it. Yesterday he complained of feeling tired and went to bed in the evening. He left strict instructions with the manservant to call him for dinner — but if he were asleep, to let him stay asleep and not bother him. Well, he was asleep, so the servant says. He saw him in bed, and tip-toed out again.'

Gossage asked: 'Does anybody benefit from Darnworth's death?'

'I don't know, sir. I don't see how we can know until the will is proved.'

2

Gossage got to his feet and strolled over to the window, so that his complete attire became visible. He was dressed in a golfing suit and the green tie looked less sensational when matched with the green socks clinging to his muscular calves. He was a powerfully built man, five feet 10 tall, hardly any neck, and prosperously wide around the equator.

'I kept the key to the study, sir, after locking it,' Craddock said, putting it on the desk. 'There may be another one in the manor, but I'll have to risk that. I also told the folks they could carry on normally, but just the same I left two men on the watch, pending your further orders.'

Gossage gave a snort. 'I was going to plant some liliums this weekend — first week in November's the right time. Now instead I'll have to hie me to Godalming and find out what all this is about.'

Craddock got to his feet.

'Naturally, sir, you'll want me to work with you?'

'Why should I?' Gossage asked blandly, putting the study key in his pocket.

'Well, since I was called to — '

'I don't want you, or the local Inspector, or even the Angel Gabriel. You should know by now that I work with only one man — Sergeant Harry Blair. That's he in the corner. Or didn't you ever hear of a chief inspector and sergeant working on their own?'

'Of course,' Craddock assented stolidly. 'Very often done, in fact, but —'

'You divisional boys are usually jealous of a chief inspector invading your territory. You'll only tolerate an area superintendent, and that because you have to. So, since you are stumped enough to come running for me you can stay out — and if I need you I'll be after you quick enough . . .'

'Yes, sir. As you say, sir.'

Gossage looked across at Blair. 'Harry, ring up Darnworth Manor and tell 'em we'll be over to stay, arriving by lunch time. If we get nothing else out of it the country air will do us good. And Harry — dig out my murder bag from the locker, will you?'

Sergeant Blair nodded and lifted the telephone. Craddock began to move away.

'I'll be seeing you again then, sir. Always glad to help in any way.'

It was 11 o'clock when Chief Inspector Gossage and Sergeant Blair came within sight of their destination, after a fast drive through wet countryside. The house was apparently in the middle of a field and surrounded by bare, wintry-looking trees.

'That be it, I wonder?' he asked, and Sergeant Blair studied it with profound disfavor.

'Could be, sir — and, if it is, I'm not much impressed.' He shook his head dubiously. 'Looks like one of those spookholes you see on the pictures — '

Sergeant Blair turned into a lane and the car sped between hedges with sodden pastureland behind them. They passed a muddy-looking pond, a solitary tree with a branch like a bent elbow bending drearily over it — and bore left to discover that the residence was not in the middle of a field, but had quite extensive grounds about it, guarded by a high brick wall with a spiked iron railing on top of it. It was the undulation of the landscape that had conveyed the wrong impression.

Blair stopped the car outside closed, wrought iron gates. He nodded to the stone pillars supporting them where, apparently of recent execution, there had been chiseled the words Darnworth Manor.

Blair sounded his horn and presently a man in oilskins appeared behind the gates.

'Well? What d'y' want?'

'Open up the gate!' Blair ordered. 'You knew we were coming. I'm Sergeant Blair and I have Chief Inspector Gossage with me.'

'All right,' the man conceded heavily. 'I'll let y'in.'

When the gates had been drawn back, Blair drove up the fairly long curving driveway to the front door, on either side of which stood a constable in cape and helmet under the sheltering portico. The door itself was of weather-stained oak with a griffin knocker.

Gossage heaved himself out, nodding to the constables as they saluted. Then he turned as the apparition in the long oilskin coat came running up through the drizzle.

Gossage could descry a thin, stern, lantern-jawed face with hollows under high cheekbones, sharply questioning gray eyes, and a very long, acquisitive nose.

'I'm Preston, the handyman,' the apparition explained.

Gossage said: 'Well, you might get the bags out of the car and then put it in the garage.'

'I'll see y'in the house first.'

Preston hurried ahead up the steps and banged on the griffin knocker.

'It'll help a bit, y'see, if I fix things up,' he added rather ambiguously. 'The old lady's very strict on who comes and who doesn't, but it's all right if I say so. Good job I heard y'first — tootin' y'horn out there. I was around the back getting some coke for the boilers.'

Gossage passed no comment, chiefly because he couldn't think of one. The immense trust apparently placed in this emaciated being was something that baffled him.

The door opened and a tall, somber, black-haired manservant of uncertain age stood with his hand on the latch. He was bent slightly in the middle as though half recovered from a blow in the stomach.

'Chief Inspector Gossage,' Preston explained to him. 'Let him in, Andrews — an' the sergeant. They're all right. I've checked up on them.'

The manservant raised his thin nose slightly as though he had detected a disagreeable odour and then waved a graceful hand into the hall.

'If you will step inside, inspector?'

Gossage glanced back at Preston, diving down the steps to help Blair with the bags. 'Thanks, Andrews.'

He took off his cap and mackintosh and handed them over with his walking stick. In polite, frosted silence the manservant allowed his gaze to rest for a fraction of a second on the convict-haircut and flaming red complexion, then he coughed gently to himself and waited while Blair set down two bags inside the front door, and Preston the remaining one.

'I presume Mrs. Darnworth knows of — '

'The mistress has made all arrangements, sir, yes.' Andrews cut Gossage short with frigid politeness. He took Blair's hat and coat and went with them to a massive oak wardrobe at the other side of the hall; then he led the way into a lounge.

'Chief Inspector Gossage and Sergeant Blair, madam,' he announced, raising his voice a trifle.

There was no answer, but evidently everything was according to plan, for he retired and closed the double doors. Gossage ran his palm over his plushy head and glanced about the big, comfortable room with its old-fashioned oaken beam ceiling and bay window looking out on to the grayness of the November day.

Then he noticed Blair's eyebrows raised in puzzled inquiry.

'Do you think, sir, that we're alone?' he asked, frowning.

'Of course you are not alone!' a voice answered him sharply from the far end of the room. 'Come over here where I can see you, and don't stand behind me talking in whispers!'

Gossage strolled forward, pausing as he rounded a deep armchair near the built-up fireplace. A small, keen, little woman was sitting on the cushioned depths, regarding him. One thin, veined hand was clenched on the chair arm while the other played with a slender gold chain looped down her black dress.

'Madam . . . ' Gossage acknowledged gravely. 'I am Chief Inspector — '

'Yes, yes. I know who you are.'

Cold blue eyes looked up at Blair.

'This young man is Sergeant Blair, I take it?

'Yes, ma'am,' Blair said.

The woman went on: 'You will forgive me not rising to greet you. You may or may not be aware that I am an invalid

— a paralytic. To rise is a physical impossibility.'

'You have my sympathy, madam,' Gossage assured her.

'I don't need it, thank you. Only the weak need sympathy . . . Sit down.'

The chief inspector pulled up a chair and in the few seconds before the woman spoke again he had a chance for a closer scrutiny.

Craddock's guess of 58 had been about right. Her face was deeply lined around the mouth and eyes, largely perhaps from physical suffering. She was spare, small-limbed, but with tremendous determination in the set of her chin and the completely fearless look in her bright blue eyes. Her hair, black in the center and gray at the sides, was drawn low over her ears and fastened in some obscure coiffure at the back of her neck.

'You don't look like a policeman, Mr. Gossage,' she commented.

'Neither did Charlie Peace look like a murderer, madam, until they found him out,' Gossage beamed on her. 'Judge not by the outside of the parcel.'

Her Roman nose wrinkled in an inaudible sniff.

'Inspector, I don't wish you to relax your efforts until you find out who murdered my husband and have him hanged. I told that divisional inspector, whose chief ability seemed to lie in tearing up carpets and floorboards in search of a weapon, that I wanted Scotland Yard on the job and if possible, less confusion.'

'Oh,' Gossage said, 'so that was why he called on me? Usually Divisional Inspector Craddock is pretty sure of his own territory.'

' 'The man made himself an infernal nuisance. We were turned out of our rooms while he conducted a night-long search.'

'I trust,' Gossage said, in a softly placating voice, 'that you will forgive me inviting the sergeant and myself. This place seems so out of the world, and our work is likely to be so confined to the Manor, that I considered a hotel in Godalming hardly fitted the case . . . '

'You are perfectly welcome to stay here

as long as necessary. Now, what do you wish to know?'

'Frankly — and I hope this doesn't surprise you, madam — I'd like to know when we might have lunch?'

Mrs. Darnworth's small, hard-lipped mouth opened wider by the briefest fraction.

'Lunch!'

'You see two hungry men, madam,' Gossage spread his hands half apologetically. 'And, as Napoleon once said, an army marches on its stomach. As far as I am concerned, and I'm sure the sergeant agrees with me, so does Scotland Yard.'

'Well, of course, you have had a journey out here,' Mrs. Darnworth admitted. 'But somehow I had expected that — What kind of an investigator are you, inspector?'

He smiled cheerfully. 'I'm sure there are no details regarding your husband's death which won't keep until after a meal.'

'Very well,' she conceded. 'I presume you have your own methods of working and I have no wish to upset them. I have given instructions for lunch to be prepared for you and the sergeant, and Andrews will direct you to the dining-room. I hope you will not think it discourteous if nobody joins you. I always have lunch in my room upstairs with Louise, who is upstairs now. My younger daughter has hers in the summer house. Mr. Crespin has been called to London. My elder daughter is out all day, but will be at home tomorrow — Sunday. Mr. Bride will be out until evening. He's gone to his Godalming home to make new arrangements concerning his work, necessitated by the death of my husband.'

3

The chief inspector was smiling good-humouredly.

'Which seems to take care of everybody, doesn't it.'

'You've no objections, have you?'

'None.'

'I'm glad of that. Divisional Inspector Craddock was of the opinion that there was nothing to be gained by confining everybody to the house. He suggested we continue our normal activities — for the time being — and left two policemen on guard. He had my husband's body removed to the mortuary in Godalming for a postmortem.'

'Well,' said Gossage, 'we'll have lunch and a chat later on?'

'It will be this evening,' Jessica Darnworth told him. 'I rest most afternoons. And as long as you are here you are at perfect liberty to do whatever you wish. I will advise Preston — whom you may regard as my personal body-guard — that you are to have carte blanche.'

'Thank you,' Gossage said. 'That will be a great help.'

'Press the bell over there. Andrews will attend to you.'

Blair did the necessary, and presently Andrews appeared in the doorway.

'You rang madam?'

'Rang?' Jessica Darnworth hooted. 'Of course I didn't! How could I get out of this chair to ring? Don't be a fool, Andrews!'

'No, madam. Sorry, madam.'

'And don't stand talking behind my back! Come round here and face me, can't you? That's better. Show the inspector and sergeant to their rooms, Andrews, and then see that they have lunch.'

'With pleasure, madam. Will there be anything else?'

'Yes. Send Preston in here. I want him to carry me up to my room.'

Andrews inclined his polished dark head and then strode to the doors and held them open as Gossage and Blair went out ahead of him. At the foot of the immense old-fashioned staircase with its thick, predominantly red carpet running down the center, Andrews paused.

'I have had your bags taken up to your rooms, gentlemen,' he announced gravely. 'If you will follow me?'

On the way up the stairs Gossage said: 'Andrews, why does the younger Miss Darnworth have her lunch in the summer house in this weather?'

'The term, sir,' Andrews said, as they came up to an immense corridor illumined with stained glass windows, 'is used a trifle loosely by the family. The summer house is a brick structure. At one time the master used it as his workshop for his hobby of — er — tinkering. Then when he gave it up Miss Sheila took it over. She spends a great deal of her time there.'

'Doing what? Tinkering?'

'She — writes, sir.'

'You mean she writes books?'

'I understand so, sir. But to the best of my knowledge none of them have achieved publication. May I show you your rooms?'

After freshening up, Gossage and Blair were halfway to the staircase along the corridor outside when a figure came hurrying up from below. She was of average height, painfully thin, with elbows so sharp it was surprising they didn't drive holes through the sleeves of the woolen dress she was wearing. She slowed to a halt as the two men advanced toward her.

'The companion help, I'd say,' Blair murmured.

'Good morning,' the woman greeted them, bobbing her small, mousy head with its flat waveless hair. Then she considered them with brown eyes set well back in a pale face.

''Morning,' Gossage acknowledged. 'You'll be Louise, I suppose?'

Again the swift, jerky curtsy. 'Yes, sir. Louise. Mrs. Darnworth's companion-help. You're here to find out how the master was killed, are you not? Mrs. Darnworth was telling me. You'll be Inspector Gossage?'

'In the flesh,' the chief inspector acknowledged. 'I'll have a chat with you later.'

'Yes, sir,' she breathed, and fled away along the corridor like a wraith, vanishing in one of the bedroom doorways.

While eating lunch Gossage questioned Andrews.

'Been here long?' he asked.

'Ten years, sir — ever since the master took over this place.'

'I gather that this is a pretty old manor house which Mr. Darnworth brought up to date?'

'Yes, sir. It was very decrepit. However, the master and his money soon wrought changes.'

'Let's have your version of what happened last night.'

'Well, sir, I sounded the gong for dinner at 8 o'clock in the usual way, and all the family assembled, with the other two gentlemen —'

'Suppose,' Gossage interrupted, 'you enumerate them.'

Blair drew a notebook out of his pocket and laid it beside his plate and began to inscribe shorthand as Andrew spoke.

'Seated here, sir, at this very table,' Andrews said, 'were Mrs. Darnworth, Miss Sheila, Miss Elaine, Mr. Crespin and Mr. Bride. They waited for the master to come in, a thing he had never failed to do punctually at 8 o'clock. But he didn't. So Mrs. Darnworth instructed me to go and inform him that the gong had sounded. I tried by knocking on the study door, which was locked as usual— '

'As usual?' Gossage gave a sharp look. 'It was, then, the custom of Mr. Darnworth to lock his study door?'

'From 7 to 8, sir, yes. He did it every night in the entire 10 years I have been here — excepting those rare occasions when he was away, of course.'

'Have you any idea why he did that?'

'I think,' Andrews answered, 'it was more or less a habit. As I recall, when I first came here, his daughters — then 15 and 12 — had the habit of bursting in on him while he was engaged in the study of market reports and similar matters connected with his business as a financier. To stop this he locked the door — and persisted in doing so right up to the time of his death.'

Gossage's eyes were thoughtful behind his glasses, then at length he began nodding to himself.

'Was the study locked when Mr. Darnworth was not using it?'

'Oh, no, sir.'

'I see. And what is all this I hear about key-wangling last night?'

'The mistress instructed me to joggle the key out of the other side of the lock. I did so, and by putting a newspaper under the door — there is plenty of room for it — and catching the fallen key on it, drew it beyond the door. By the time I had done this everybody had joined me at the study door, even Mrs. Darnworth in her wheel-chair.'

'And nobody went outside and tried by the window?'

'Preston did sir — but the curtains were drawn across it and the mistress was against smashing the window until she was sure what had happened. The key-wangling seemed to offer the best opportunity with the least damage. Anyway, when he got into the study we — '

'Found Mr. Darnworth dead with a wound in the back of his skull. I know. I understand the lights were on?'

'They were, sir, yes. The twin lights of the electrolier, and the desk light.'

'M'm . . . Do you know if Mr. Darnworth had changed the appointments of the study much? I mean, was he addicted to altering the positions of the furniture? Some men are, and women all the time.'

Andrews shook his head. 'He didn't change the arrangement of the study in all the time he used it, sir.'

Blair had time for three mouthfuls and then the chief inspector started off again.

'Where were the other people in the house at the time of Mr. Darnworth's death? Medical evidence says he died at about 7.30.'

'For myself, sir, I was as usual in the servants' quarters — which can be verified, of course. Mrs. Darnworth was in her room with Louise, dressing for dinner. Preston, whom you have met, was upstairs in the corridor, waiting to carry the mistress downstairs. Miss Elaine had not come in from the vet's — '

'The vet's?' Gossage repeated.

Andrews gave a grave little smile. 'Miss Elaine is one of those very strong-minded young women, inordinately fond of animals, and she spends all her days helping Mr. Findley, the veterinary surgeon in the village, attend his animals. The task is self-imposed. Miss Elaine does it for the love of it, not as a paid employee. She had not come home yesterday evening at 7.30. It was a quarter to 8 when she arrived, in the company of Mr. Bride.'

'He'd been out, then?'

'He arrived here in his car, with luggage, at 4.30, and went out again at 5.30 saying he was going to meet Miss Elaine.'

'I see. He was away just over two hours, then?' Gossage proceeded in silence with his lunch for an interval, then he went on: 'About Mr. Crespin? I understand he was asleep following a repair to the radio the previous night?'

Andrews said: 'He left the house about 6. I heard him say to Miss Sheila that he felt 'cobwebby' — yes, I'm sure that was the expression — and that a walk in the fresh air would do him good. Just before 7 he was back again and rang for me. He said he was going up to his room to get some sleep. At half-past 7 I was to remind him about dinner. He said that if he had fallen asleep I was not to awaken him and that he would have some refreshment when he awakened and would not bother with dinner.'

'And?' Gossage inquired.

'I went in his room at 7.30. He had left the door unlocked. He was in bed, his back turned to me. I could just see his hair above the quilt and he was breathing deeply . . . In fact, I believe he was snoring.'

'You believe he was? Can't you be sure?'

Andrews straightened momentarily and nodded. 'Yes, sir, I am sure he was,' he said gravely.

The chief inspector looked absently at

his half-completed lunch.

'Yet he came down to dinner?'

'Yes, he came down in a hurry at the last moment. I presume he must have awakened just in time.'

Sergeant Blair put down his pencil with quiet rebellion and began to catch up on his lunch. He nearly had time to finish before Gossage emerged from a brown study.

'I understand Miss Sheila was playing the piano? For how long was it?'

'Nearly an hour, sir — 7 to 8. In the music room across the hall.'

'Mr. Darnworth concentrated on figures and business matters with a piano playing in the next room? I admire his powers of detachment.'

Andrews looked surprised for a moment.

'That aspect never seemed to enter into it, sir. Miss Sheila is a most accomplished pianist with a distinct leaning towards the classics. Besides, the walls in this house are extremely thick. I doubt if her playing would have been more than a murmur when heard from the study.'

'Which could account for nobody anywhere hearing the sound of the shot which killed Mr. Darnworth?'

'I would suggest it was a likely possibility, sir.'

4

'Well, thanks, Andrews. You've been most helpful. I think I'll take a little stroll around the house. The study, to begin with. Now where's that key?'

He fished in his waistcoat pocket and nodded as he brought the key in view. Blair, catching his look, got up and joined him. Andrews directed them across the hall to a closed door not far from the foot of the staircase, and on the same side as the lounge.

'This, sir, is the music-room,' he said, swinging the door open. 'And next to it is the master's study. Will that be all now?'

'For the moment,' Gossage assented, and he waddled into the music-room and stood looking about him.

Predominant among the furniture was a polished black grand piano with the top raised and the keyboard lid closed. Before it was a square stool with a red satin seat. Upon the floor was expensive carpet fitted with exactness.

By the single bay window was a china cabinet. On the opposite wall an old fashioned note was struck in the shape of an antique whatnot. Otherwise the appointments were commonplace — easy chairs, divan, a tall reading lamp, and, gold-painted to make it appear less conspicuous, a steam heating pipe stood where the fireplace had been.

Gossage strolled over to the piano and raised the keyboard lid, tapped out a few bars of 'Danny Boy' on the white keys with one finger and then lowered the lid back again. His thoughtful gaze moved to the wall that divided the room from the study and then traveled back to the window.

'This window can be opened, sir,' Blair remarked, nodding to it. 'I'm not hoping to explain anything away,' he added. 'I'm just trying to form a hypothesis. Do you think Miss Sheila might have — well, done something? Connected with the murder?'

Gossage raised an eyebrow. 'How?'

'As I say, I don't know — but she was

nearest her father when he died. Right next door to him.' Blair, pursuing a thought deeply rooted in his mind, pushed the window open amidst a shower of raindrops and leaned outside. To the right, about 15 feet away, was the window of the lounge; to the left, about the same distance, was the window of the study. Midway between music-room window and study window was a strong iron rain pipe from the roof. Both windows had fairly broad ledges and the lounge a rather smaller one.

'I wonder,' said Blair, 'if Miss Sheila could, by gripping the rain pipe, perhaps jump from this window to the study window.'

'Could she now?' Gossage sounded quite tolerant and his smile was beamingly encouraging. Then he blew through his pipe and knocked the bowl gently on the windowsill outside.

'I repeat, she could . . . ' Blair was becoming heavily emphatic, which was a sure sign he was excited. 'That would do away with the need of footprints on the soft flower bed here.' He leaned through the open window again and jabbed a finger downward significantly. 'Once at the study window, she opened it or probably had left it unlatched in readiness during the day. We heard from Andrews that the study is unlocked when not in use. Anybody could go into it.'

'You're doing fine,' the chief inspector approved, filling his pipe from the pouch. 'Then what did she do?'

'Shot her father, left the way she'd entered, and drew the window catch into place after her. There are plenty of ways of locking a window from the outside.'

'But, Harry,' the inspector said, 'all this assumes that Sheila climbed a ladder to shoot her father, or else hung like a monkey from, say, the electrolier.'

'Why should she do that?'

'The shot came from above.'

'Oh,' Sergeant Blair said, and looked vaguely irritated.

'Can't gainsay facts,' Gossage told him. 'And in any case Darnworth would hardly sit motionless while his daughter came through the study window with an air rifle. How'd she carry the air rifle without it hindering her movements? What kept the piano playing while she did the deed?'

'Sorry, sir. Just a theory, anyway.'

'And why do you imagine Sheila would wish to kill her father?'

''I relied on your observation for that, sir — that nobody seems to care much now he's dead. A girl who'll shut herself away and write when her father's been bumped off is — well, pretty callous, if you ask me.'

'Suppose,' Gossage said, smiling, 'we stop jumping to conclusions and get things a bit more in focus first? Let's take a look at the study.'

Taking the study key from his pocket, he turned it in the lock and swung the door open. The first things that became evident were the smell of stale cigar smoke and heavy darkness.

Gossage switched on the electrolier. 'No curtains drawn back. Hop over and draw them aside, Harry.'

Blair did so and the pallid November daylight came into the room. Gossage switched the lights off again and then for a while stood on the threshold.

Blair, from the opposite end of the study, looked about him, too. Near to him, by the window, was the desk, average-sized, its leather-topped surface littered with financial papers, market reports and correspondence. There were ink wells, red and black, in a mahogany stand, a telephone, and a desk light.

From Gossage's point of view by the door, the desk was at the other end of the room, a distance of about 20 feet. On his left was the bureau, then came the floor-to-ceiling shelves lined with books; then the window behind Blair, and the desk. On the other wall were the hard-backed chairs, two easy chairs and a big Jacobean bookcase filled carelessly with manuals and periodicals.

Gossage sniffed the air again. Despite the fact that he was smoking himself, he could still detect the odor of cigar fumes. When he reached the desk he looked at the ash tray. A little heap of ash lay in it and the end of a cigar.

'Evidently the old man smoked a good deal, sir,' Blair commented, coming round the desk. 'You know how a room gets to hold the smell of tobacco fumes no matter how much you try and freshen it up.'

Gossage nodded. 'Not that it matters. Smoker or non-smoker he was shot dead: that's our problem. Let's have a look at the window.'

They moved over to the window and promptly received their first punch in the nose. In particular did Sergeant Blair look discomfited, and with good reason. The window was of the non-opening variety, a solid frame of mullioned panes.

'Blast!' Blair murmured. 'No wonder Craddock said the window was one of the type you can't tamper with! I never thought of a solid one.'

'I did,' Gossage grinned. 'It was in his report which I read over to myself. Sorry, Harry; I should have told you when you were waltzing away with your masterly theory regarding Sheila.'

'This kicks the bottom out of that theory, sir. She couldn't have got in here.'

'No, by gosh, and neither could anybody else!' Gossage tapped his teeth edge with his pipe. 'This rules the window right out, Harry. Puts a blue pencil clean through it. All it does do is explain the stale air in here. Lack of adequate ventilation.'

Gossage began to prowl round the room, taking his time, examining everything with an intense thoroughness.

Finally, he stood contemplating the oak paneled ceiling with the electrolier depending from the center, about 10 feet away from the desk. It was fitted with a copper rosette flush with the ceiling; then it came down in a single copper tube, and where the branching occurred, was a second rosette of a lighter-hued copper than the one in the ceiling.

'I'll be hanged if I can understand it, sir . . .'

Gossage gave a little start and looked at the sergeant.

'What did you say, Harry?'

'I said I can't understand it, sir. This business doesn't make sense. There's no position from which anybody could have shot Darnworth, and even less explanation of how anybody could have got in and out of the room and left the only key on the inside.

Gossage smiled good-humouredly. 'Harry, don't let it throw you. Fit the parts into place and the solution will be self-evident. We're not going to batter out what few brains we've got trying to solve how somebody got in and out of here. We're going to fit the parts.'

'Yes, sir. In what way?'

'First of all,' the chief inspector said, 'let's grab hold of something we do know. That is: Darnworth died from a slug from a B.S.A. air rifle. No getting round that. But we can't find the rifle — or at any rate Craddock couldn't. And Craddock is intensely thorough. If he says he had this place searched from top to bottom — which Mrs. Darnworth verifies — and couldn't find the weapon, we can be pretty sure it isn't in the house.'

'We-ll, yes,' Blair agreed slowly. 'Even Craddock isn't infallible though, sir. It might have been hidden so neatly that it would be hard to find. Might take weeks.'

Gossage shrugged heavy shoulders. 'Ask yourself a question. If you'd murdered a man with a fairly cumbersome thing like a B.S.A. air rifle, a difficult weapon to keep right, would you keep it in the house, knowing the house would be searched. And remember that after the murder nobody left the house until Craddock had searched it, and two policemen have been on guard during the night. You can't walk out of the house with a bulky thing like an air rifle without showing some sign of it.'

'You might, sir, carrying it under a long mackintosh like that one worn by Preston. It might have been got out that way.'

'Yes, but not until this morning. Nobody went out until then. Which brings me back to my first belief, Harry. Assuming that somebody in the house did it — which seems more than likely — I'd say the best way to be rid of the rifle would be to throw it from the house as far as possible. Then, after leaving the house, reclaim it.'

Gossage seemed to make up his mind suddenly.

'I'm going for a ramble and while I'm

about it I'll have a word with Craddock. too. I'd suggest you have a word with those two constables and find out from them what each person leaving here this morning was wearing. Then dismiss them: they don't need to stay on any longer. In that way you can perhaps clear up your own theory and I'll see what I can do with mine.'

'Right, sir. I believe it's a good 10 miles to Inspector Craddock's headquarters.'

'Who cares? Nothing like exercise.'

* * *

The Chief Inspector set off, his mackintosh over his shoulder and his snake-headed stick gripped firmly in his hand.

As he walked down the drive, he stopped, turned, and studied the front of the manor.

To the left of the front door were the bay windows of the dining-room; to the right of it were the single bay windows of lounge, music-room, and study. Above, there were six windows, mullioned, the first on the left he identified as belonging to Blair's bedroom, and the next — to the right and nearly over the front door — as his own. The others he had yet to place.

His gaze traveled above the bedroom windows to the long iron gutter and its three down pipes — then upward to the lofty, sloping-roof, slated in the modern style, with an old fashioned and now disused massive chimney in the center.

'Hello! Looking the old place over?'

Gossage twirled round. He had been so absorbed in his study of the manor's façade he had not heard the footfalls along the gravel. He faced a young woman in dark maroon slacks and a canary-colored woolen jumper with a polo collar.

'Did I startle you?' she asked, smiling.

5

Gossage took off his cap, assessing the girl quickly.

'Matter of fact, you did,' he admitted. His eyes wandered to the bulky file she was carrying under her arm. 'You'll be Miss Darnworth, I take it? Miss Sheila Darnworth?'

She nodded. She was good looking in a sensitive way, her nose spoiling the effect somewhat by being a trifle too long. She had a well-shaped, generous mouth, a pointed chin, and smoky gray eyes that looked tired because of heavy lids. She was hatless, her blonde hair blowing a little in the damp breeze.

'Yes, I'm Sheila Darnworth,' she assented, having appraised the red face. cropped head, and gold-rimmed glasses. 'Let me make a guess. You're the chief inspector. Frankly, I forget the name.'

'Gossage.'

'That's it. I had just heard about your

phone call when I left the house this morning. You won't think me awfully rude for not having come into the house to meet you, will you?'

Gossage smiled a little. 'To be quite truthful, young lady, I don't blame you. I never heard of anybody being anxious to meet an Inspector from Scotland Yard.'

She considered him, head a trifle on one side.

'You know, you don't look a bit like what I expected. I'd sort of anticipated a square-jawed man in a bowler hat — keeping it on in the house, too! You're so — different! More like an uncle, or something, or a squire.'

She looked suddenly guilty. 'I say — don't stand bareheaded because of me, please. I appreciate it, but there's really no need. I'm used to being without a hat and it makes me forget some people aren't.'

'Very considerate of you, Miss.'

Gossage put his cap back on again and pulled it low over his eyes. Raising his stick, he considered the snake's head, then his gaze went back to the sharply revealed lines of Sheila Darnworth's 22-year-old figure. Andrews had said she had been 12 ten years ago . . .Yes — 22.

'Do you think you could spare a few moments for a chat, Miss Darnworth?' Gossage asked. 'I'm going for a stroll, but since I've met you I might as well talk now as later — unless you're busy?'

'Busy? No, not now.'

Gossage began walking slowly and she kept in step beside him. She had lithe, easy strides, he noticed — and rather long legs for her approximate five-feet-five of height.

'I believe you write?' he said. 'Over in the brick summer house yonder?'

'Yes. I write murder thrillers,' she said.

Gossage's eyes widened.

'Do you, by gosh? Now that does intrigue me!'

'You're very polite,' she said, smiling seriously. 'You can laugh outright if you want, you know. Most people do. My mother, my sister — and my father laughed more than anybody. I suppose there is something funny about a girl like me writing murders. But, Mr. Gossage, you said you wanted a chat with me. About my father, do you mean? And — and the dreadful thing that happened to him?'

'Yes. I'd like your side of it.'

'I told everything to the divisional inspector last night. There isn't anything more.'

'Oh, you never can tell.' Gossage smiled at her encouragingly. 'You were playing the piano for an hour last evening from 7 to 8?'

'I was, yes. But there was nothing unusual in that. I've done it for years every evening between 7 and 8. I call it my practice hour.'

'Did you during that time hear anything unusual? Say, a shot — or a cry from your father? Anything at all. Not while you were playing you wouldn't, of course, but you might have during the rests.'

'I didn't hear anything,' she said, shrugging.

'Do you know if your father had any enemies?'

'Not to my knowledge. He may have

had some in business, of course. As you probably know by now, he was a pretty influential man in the financial world. It is an unfortunate fact that he was not greatly liked.'

'Any more than he was at home, apparently,' Gossage said.

'I don't think I quite understand what you mean by that, Mr. Gossage,' the girl said.

He smiled. 'Not one of you, as far as I can make out, has deviated from normal pursuits. Of course I do not expect you to go about in sackcloth and ashes, but somehow I'm old-fashioned enough to expect, perhaps, dark clothes, a brief cessation of work in respect to the dead. Only your mother is wearing black.'

'She always wears black,' the girl said; then she looked down at herself quickly in her canary yellow jumper and maroon slacks.

'Do you know . . . ' she paused awkwardly. 'I never thought of it! I always wear these duds to work in — after all, Mr. Gossage, work goes on.'

'I agree that ordinary employment goes

on, but . . . ' The chief inspector spread his hands. 'You are your own mistress in this — this writing you do; your sister, I understand, only helps the local vet because it pleases her to do it. I exclude Mr. Crespin and Mr. Bride because they are not of the family, Look, Miss Darnworth,' he broke off seriously, 'I get the perfectly obvious impression that it doesn't much matter to you or your sister — or maybe your mother — whether your father is dead. Am I right?'

Sheila Darnworth hesitated for a long moment then she gave a firm little nod.

'Yes. You're right,' she assented. 'It makes it a good deal easier now my father's gone. He was not the kind of man with whom one could get along. I respected him as a daughter should, but I have the right to say that he didn't conform to my idea of what a father should be. For instance, if he were not dead I wouldn't be carrying this file of mine into the house, in case he should find it. As it is, I can. Understand?'

Gossage filled his pipe slowly from his pouch as he regarded her. Then gradually the smile came back on his red face.

'I'm not going to poke my nose in, Miss Darnworth,' Gossage told her. They were at the gates, and he added: 'Oh, before we part. 'This young man you're engaged to — '

'You mean Barry Crespin?'

'Yes. When can I see him? I believe he went off to the city on business.'

'That,' the girl said, 'was quite unexpected. He's a radio engineer — has two stores of his own in London. They rang up this morning to say there was something urgent that only he could attend to. So off he went in his car. You'll like Barry, inspector. I'd do anything to help him because I'm sure he deserves it. He's one of those sort of boys who gets what he wants.'

'Well, glad to have had this little chat, Miss Darnworth,' Gossage said. 'See you about the house, I expect. Now I think I'll give myself some exercise.'

She nodded and lifted the catch on the gate for him. With a nod of thanks he strode out into the lane and began to walk with the steady, deliberate tread which had earned him his title of 'The Crimson Rambler.'

When he returned to the manor just after darkness had fallen Gossage found himself confronted in the hall by a woman who couldn't be anybody else but Elaine Darnworth.

'I suppose you are Inspector Gossage? Just the man I want to see!'

For a woman Elaine Darnworth was tall beyond the average, dressed in jodhpurs, riding boots, a tweed jacket and green silk shirt with a gold pin through an emerald colored tie. She was holding a riding crop that she thwacked with a certain menacing intentness against her leg. It crossed Gossage's mind that Andrews had been right. Here, definitely, was a very strong-willed woman,

'Is something the matter, Miss Darnworth?' Gossage sounded quite placid.

'Matter!' she exclaimed, 'I should think so! What do you mean by turning this place into an exhibition piece? What are all those men doing plowing up the gardens with their elephantine boots? Is this the best way in which you can conduct an investigation?'

Her face had something of Sheila's pointedness about the chin, but there the sisterly resemblance stopped. She was darkly handsome, full lipped to the point of arrogance, with a wealth of dark and tumbling hair. Her eyes were intensely blue. Pride, possessiveness and ruthless will were all there, fighting each other.

Gossage said: 'You are an intelligent woman, Miss Darnworth, and — It is Miss Darnworth?'

'I am Elaine Darnworth, yes.'

'Well, you are intelligent enough to realize that we have to find the weapon with which your father was shot. It isn't in the house and so we are looking outside.'

'And why on earth should you expect it to be there? That it can't be found in the house is surely sufficient guarantee that it isn't going to be found?'

'By no means.' Gossage regarded her levelly. 'By no means, Miss Darnworth,' he repeated. 'As far as I am concerned the search will go on. We're going to find that weapon.'

'I object to you making the manor a target for gossip.'

'Murder,' Gossage said, 'has an unpleasant habit of drawing attention to itself. However, I think you are worrying needlessly. By the way, I understand you are engaged to Mr. Bride?'

'Yes. Which, I would add, has nothing whatever to do with my father's death.'

'He meets you every night as you leave your self-imposed task as assistant to Mr. Findley, does he not?'

'He most certainly does. It is not altogether safe for a woman to be alone in these lonely parts after dark.'

'He doesn't, Miss Darnsworth. I've been checking up. Mr. Bride has never been anywhere near the veterinary's, and Mr. Findley certainly doesn't know of him.'

'I am not in the habit,' said Elaine Darnworth, 'of discussing my private affairs with Mr. Findley! And — '

'Miss Darnworth, in your statement to the police you said that last night Mr. Bride met you at the vet's and came home with you. Bride verified that fact in his statement. Now I find that you hadn't met Mr. Bride even after you had got a mile away from the vet's. I really must insist on having the real facts.'

'I think you're trying to read something into my statement which isn't there,' she said. 'Something suspicious. I might have expected it of a detective.'

Gossage shrugged, unmoved.

'You and Mr. Bride were the only two persons absent from the manor when your father met his death. You came in together 15 minutes after his death — which by medical evidence has been placed as 7.30. What did happen yesterday evening?'

There was a silence as Elaine reflected. Then a man's voice, rather high pitched but definitely languid, spoke from the doorway of the lounge.

'You'd better explain it, Elly. Playing ducks and drakes with the police never did anybody any good. Not because the police are smarter than anybody else but because they have the preponderance of power. 'Evening, Inspector Gossage.'

6

While speaking, the man had walked across the hall — a squarely built youngish fellow with a good forehead and fair hair. He had an expression that was neither surprised nor supercilious; it was hard to tell. The main impression he gave was of mental and physical strength at the cost of good looks. In general his features were blunt — a peg-top nose, an upper lip too long, and gray eyes much too closely set.

'Evening,' Gossage responded, nodding. 'Mr. Bride?'

'Gregory Bride, yes. Miss Darnworth is simply being obstinate. Habit she's got. I've told her about it many a time but she never seems to learn. There's no mystery, inspector. I've never been to the vet's to meet her — not right to the vet's, that is. When I said that last night to the divisional inspector — and Elly here said it, too — I used the term loosely.'

'I see,' Gossage said. 'I'd suggest you be a trifle more accurate in your statements henceforth, Mr. Bride'

'Yes, suppose I'd better,' Bride admitted. 'Anyway, I've always kept clear of Findley's place because Miss Darnworth asked me to. She just doesn't want Findley or anybody else outside the family to know that she's engaged. Not, mind you, because she's ashamed of me,' Bride added, grinning and blinking again, 'but because she thinks it's cheap to discuss one's private affairs with strangers.'

'And so it is!' Elaine declared flatly, and the crop banged viciously. 'And see here, inspector, I only became engaged to Mr. Bride because I wanted to help him with his scientific inventions, and it seemed to me that as his wife-to-be I'd be able to influence my father more easily than Mr. Bride himself.'

'The old man didn't like me — much,' Gregory Bride explained, showing his big crooked teeth. 'It was mutual, though. I didn't like him a bit. Too hard-boiled. Elly here is just like him, you know. Sheila is more like her mother. Or rather as I understand her mother was in the old days.'

'I think,' Gossage said, 'we are wandering from the point. So you didn't meet Miss Darnworth at the vet's. What, then, did you do?'

'Met her well clear of the village, as usual. Then we came here together. We've done it for long enough, every weekend. I'm here for the weekend, in case you're not aware of it.'

'I'm quite aware of it, Mr. Bride, thank you. I also understand that you arrived here yesterday about 4.30 from Godalming in your car, bringing your luggage — a thing you've done for some time. At 5.30 you left again to meet Miss Darnworth. You came back here with her at 7.45. At what time did you meet her, and where?'

Something of the self-assured look seemed to fade a little from Gregory Bride's face.

'We met at the fork of the lane — Manor Lane as it's called, just where it joins Bexley Road. You'll know the lane, since you must have come down it to get to the manor. It has Morgan's Deep in it.'

'You mean the pond with the tree over it?'

'That's it. We met about 25 to 6.'

'In your car, or walking?'

'Walking,' Elaine Darnworth said briefly.

'That left you two hours and five minutes to wait, then, Mr. Bride?'

'Yes. Elly was late. But I didn't mind. I was expecting Elly to turn up about 20 past 6 but she was delayed. So I just waited and strolled up and down smoking.'

Gossage said: 'It's time I freshened up after my walk. Glad to have met you two. Maybe we'll get to know each other better before long.'

With a cheerful nod he turned and went up the stairs.

Somewhat to his surprise, Gossage found Sergeant Blair in an easy chair in the bedroom.

'Glad you're back, sir.' He got up, stubbed the cigarette out in the ashtray. 'Hope you don't mind me waiting in here? I felt sort of out of it amongst that crowd downstairs. They're at tea there — in the lounge, including a big-footed dragon by the name of Elaine Darnworth.'

Gossage grinned, pulled off his jacket, and began to roll up his sleeves. Then he unpegged his pince-nez and set them down.

'Put yourself where you like, Harry. Did you find out what the folks were wearing?'

'Yes,' Blair pulled out his notebook. 'Sheila Darnworth — and a nice girl she is, too — was wearing slacks and a jumper — no raincoat or hat. She hurried through the drizzle to the 'summer house' and there stayed. Bride had on a light mackintosh, but it was flowing open and there was nothing concealed, Crespin had on a fairly long raincoat, but he dropped his cigarette case as he left the house and stooped to pick it up. He couldn't stoop if concealing a rifle under his coat, could he?'

'It would present difficulties,' Gossage agreed. 'Well, come and tell me more while I wash.'

Blair nodded and in the bathroom he had to shout to make himself heard above the swishings of water.

'Elaine Darnworth went out in a leather jacket to protect her from the rain — otherwise she was in riding habit. No place for concealing a rifle. In fact, the only one who has gone out a lot during the day has been Preston. And you know the length of that oilskin of his. He alone seems the most likely to fit my theory.'

Gossage dried himself with the towel and his face emerged like a winter sun.

'I'll tell you what you do, Harry . . . ' He winked seriously. 'Just forget all about your theory, eh? Start again? It's all right to play about with but it ignores one vital detail — the mind of the killer.'

'Oh?' Blair shut his notebook. 'How so?'

'Whoever committed this crime has ingenuity, eh?'

'I should say there's no doubt of it. Locked study and no trace of the weapon. So?'

'He — or she — being ingenious enough to kill old man Darnworth and leave no trace of it would never be clumsy enough to try and get the weapon out of the house under a mackintosh or something.'

'I don't know so much about that, sir — '

'But I do,' Gossage insisted. 'Besides, how could they know that they'd need a mackintosh or coat, anyway? Might not have rained. Might have been warm, as it sometimes is in November.' Gossage dried his arms vigorously. 'No, Barry, it doesn't fit. The person responsible would think up something just as ingenious as the act of murder itself. I admit I'm a bit woolly brained on that aspect myself, and so far the only answer that occurs to me is that the weapon was thrown from the house, probably from one of the upper windows, to be picked up later. I saw Craddock this afternoon and told him to get his boys on the job of searching for it.'

'I saw them arrive and start searching just before it got dark.'

'I don't expect them to find the air rifle because I give the murderer credit for having more brains than to have left it lying about so long — but I do maintain that footprints are possible. The rifle would have to be taken hastily. There wouldn't, as I see it, be time to obliterate footprints as well. Faint hope, maybe, but only one so far.'

He went across to the dressing table, fitted a fresh collar, and pulled his green tie into place while Blair thought the point out.

'Yes,' Blair agreed finally, with all the signs of having applied logic to the problem. 'I think you're right, sir. Being rid of that rifle under a mackintosh would be chancy . . . Incidentally, have you found out anything? During your ramble, I mean?'

'I've found that Sheila Darnworth didn't care much for her father. I've also discovered, through Sheila, that Barry Crespin is a go-ahead radio-engineer who usually gets what he wants and that Sheila is very much in love with him. Crespin has two radio stores in the city. One of his assistants rang him from London, asking him to go to the city as there was an important matter that only he could deal with. I'm having Craddock check on it. I learned from the formidable Elaine that she only became engaged to Gregory Bride so that she could push things with her father on Bride's behalf. Scientific inventions, or something, Bride says he didn't like the old man and that the dislike was mutual. I had a chat with the vet for whom Elaine works. He never heard of Gregory Bride. Last night she left the vet's at 7, whereas she usually goes about 6. He walked part of the way with her, going to a case, but Bride had not met her when he, the vet, left her at 7.20.'

'The things you pick up on a ramble, sir,' Blair observed.

Gossage got into his jacket again and clipped his pince-nez back on his nose. 'There is the matter of the queer behavior of Gregory Bride last evening. He says he waited two hours and five minutes at the fork of Manor Lane for Elaine. I suppose a man could do that — nothing impossible about it — but he'd need the hell of a lot of patience. On the other hand, you can do a lot in two hours and five minutes.'

'You can, sir, yes,' Blair agreed heavily.

'As for Elaine . . .' Gossage reflected. 'As for her, the time seems to check. She left the vet's at 7. I've made sure of that, and walking the two and a half-mile distance she got in here at 7.45, which is near as dammit.'

'And Bride didn't like old man Darnworth, eh?' Blair mused. 'Did he say why?'

'Because he was obstinate, I gathered.' Gossage grinned. 'So I thought —'

From the hall came the vibration of a gong. Blair became alert and momentarily avidity crossed his square face.

'That sounds like dinner, and I'm ready for it.'

Gossage nodded. 'Meeting adjourned, Harry. Come on.'

They left the bedroom together and arrived in the dining-room to find the family and guests assembled — six of them, every one sitting with something of the circumspect detachment of a board meeting, dominated at the head of the table by Mrs. Darnworth, still in black silk with the long loop of gold chain down her small bosom.

To Gossage's silent relief there was no sign of evening dress. The men were entirely informal in lounge suits and the two younger women were in dark blue. The change from a yellow jumper suited Sheila, but no change she could affect suited the full-breasted Elaine. She sat at the table like a pouter pigeon, her coldly suspicious eyes watching the two men as they came into the room.

'Gentlemen, you are late!' Mrs. Darnworth observed, and set her firm little mouth. 'I would remark that we are in the habit of assembling in the lounge five minutes prior to dinner so that we may all sit down together. Call us slaves of habit if you wish, but that is how it was in my husband's lifetime, and that is how I mean it to continue.'

'Very sorry,' Gossage apologized humbly, and settled in his chair; then his eyes traveled across the faultlessly laid table to the young man seated opposite him.

7

'Mr. Crespin — Inspector Gossage and Sergeant Blair.' Mrs. Darnworth made the introductions.

'Glad to know you, inspector, and you, sergeant,' Crespin said, smiling.

He was about 33 or 34, comfortably plump, and with unruly blond hair. His complexion was as delicate as a girl's and his teeth small and even. In a careless kind of way, he was quite good looking.

'You have made my list complete, Mr. Crespin,' Gossage told him. 'I've now met everybody.'

Nobody commented immediately. It looked as though they were all waiting for the chief inspector to add something, but he refrained. Instead he beamed disarmingly as he looked at each member of the party, even the washed-out Louise, looking very small and somehow squeezed in a lacy affair that emphasized her boniness.

'I trust the experience of meeting people has helped your investigation, inspector,' Elaine remarked cynically. 'It seems to me that you're not getting on very rapidly in tracing the murderer of my father.'

Gossage said: 'I'm not a miracle worker. I'm simply a paid employee of Scotland Yard and unfortunately for me clues don't hang on trees like ripe plums. And speaking of plums reminds me. Actually, I don't like talking about the murder at all . . . ' He gave a sigh and shook his scrubbed head. 'I'm a simple man who loves gardening and nature, but fate has bamboozled me into bringing villains to justice for their misdeeds.'

'While finding your brief digression into personal foibles interesting, inspector, I would like to know how far you have progressed!' Mrs. Darnworth made the observation as she fixed him with her blue eyes. 'You have met everybody: you have, I understand, been out part of the day. Now you have men wandering about the grounds with lanterns.'

'Yes,' Gossage acknowledged amiably.

'A fact of which Miss Darnworth has already reminded me.'

'That is purely because she dislikes the police as much as I do — but I have good sense to realize that you have, of necessity, to act as you see fit — '

'Heaven be praised,' Gossage murmured under his breath.

'Are we not therefore entitled to know where we stand?' Mrs. Darnworth asked.

'You stand just where you were to start with,' Gossage said. 'All of you have perfectly reasonable explanations for your actions last night: none of you seem to be aware of any enemies Mr. Darnworth might have had, and it is a complete mystery how anybody got in and out of the study to kill him, and an even bigger one whither went the weapon with which he was shot . . . '

'What did kill him?' Gregory Bride asked, 'I know he was shot in the head, but with what? Was it a revolver?'

Gossage looked round on the faces. 'It was a B.S.A. air rifle.'

'Air rifle!' Barry Crespin exclaimed. 'That puts a different complexion on things. It'd be a big thing to hide, and also it would be an easy weapon for the killer to get, much easier than a revolver, or ordinary rifle.'

Sheila asked: 'What comes next, Mr. Gossage?'

'The inquest.'

'Technically, yes,' Sheila agreed. 'I mean here. What do we do?'

Gossage smiled at her.

'My dear young lady, none of you have paused in your normal pursuits following the death of Mr. Darnworth: so why should you do so as time goes on? I'll be frank. I don't believe one of you is a bit concerned over the fact that Mr. Darnworth is dead.'

'That,' Mrs. Darnworth said, 'is an intolerable assumption, Mr. Gossage.'

He shook his head. 'I disagree. I already have it from Miss Sheila that she at least does not consider herself any the worse off by her father's demise.'

'Why should she?' Barry Crespin demanded. 'She inherits everything!'

If Barry Crespin had brought a lighted bomb from his pocket and placed it in the center of the table the effect could not have been more impressive. The color went out of Sheila's cheeks; her mother and sister turned to look at her in cold, steady interrogation. Crespin added: 'I suppose . . . '

'What are you talking about, Barry?' Mrs. Darnworth demanded of him, her voice so sharp that it hurt the ear.

'Yes, what?' Elaine snapped

'I'm only repeating what Sheila told me.'

The older woman's eyes darted to Sheila. 'And by what right do you dare assume that you are the sole beneficiary? You of all people!'

'Dad told me once. One morning when he was in a good humor. He said everything would come to me if anything ever happened to him. He added something about a proviso — '

'What proviso?' Elaine demanded.

'I don't know,' Sheila muttered, looking desperately uncomfortable. 'He wouldn't tell me. He may even have been having one of his silly jokes about the will; I don't know. But he did say that.'

'And she told me,' Crespin added. 'I didn't ask her — It was — Well, just one of those things when we were talking.'

Mrs. Darnworth went whiter and the lines became more clearly marked round her firm mouth and piercing eyes. Just for a second or two it was quite plain that towering rage was governing her; then she got herself in hand and drew a deep breath.

'I see,' she said, nearly inaudibly — and then staring before her without a trace of expression.

'All of which makes it look bad for you, Sheila,' Gregory Bride commented, grinning. 'I mean motive. Am I not right, inspector?'

'Oh, I don't know . . . ' Gossage did not seem at all perturbed. 'I might just as easily say that you had a motive, Mr. Bride. You told me you didn't like Mr. Darnworth because he was — 'too hard boiled', I think you said. And you said he didn't like you, either.'

Bride opened his mouth with its long top lip; then he shut it again and frowned over a thought.

'They're none too frank over coming into the open, are they, Mr. Gossage?' Sheila had a defiant bitterness in her expression now as she looked round the table. 'Now I seem to have taken the most likely motive for dad's death to myself, they don't tell you how much they hated dad. Not a bit of it! Little Sheila has been idiot enough to stick out her neck, so let her take the consequences.'

'Sheila!' her mother breathed harshly.

'Sorry,' the girl said, her sleepy eyes gleaming under the heavy lids, 'but I'm not going to sit here and take all the responsibility. You, mother, hated dad for one reason only — because he made you a paralytic! Five years ago he drove the car in which you had your accident and which made you — as you are. Since then you've been unbearable to all of us, and particularly to me.'

'No. I never forgave him for that,' Mrs. Darnworth admitted somberly. 'He had too much to drink that evening,' she went on, 'and I went out in the car with him against my will. He had a smash, but escaped unhurt. Since then I have been like this, never free from pain. I hated him,' she whispered, seeming to lose awareness of those about her. 'I think I had always hated him, but never so bitterly as when he caused this to happen to me. I should never have married him. I should have curbed my ambition and married Clinton Brown. He may only be a simple man without a great deal of money, living in the village because he likes the peace, but at least he is honest and kind.'

Sheila reached out a slim hand and patted her mother's arm.

'Thanks, mum,' she said gratefully. 'That takes a bit of the burden off my back. Equal motive, as it were.' Her drowsy eyes flashed a challenge at Gossage.

'Well,' he said, 'it seems to me that you two ladies are frightfully anxious to find motives for Mr. Darnworth's death. What about the rest of you?'

'As far as I'm concerned,' Barry Crespin said, 'I may as well admit that I didn't care much for Mr. Darnworth. He was too autocratic. Besides, he didn't do the right thing by Sheila. He held her up to ridicule in company too often.'

'Ridicule?' Gossage repeated.

'Barry — please!' Sheila looked at him imploringly and for a moment he hesitated; then his round, fresh-complexioned face took on sudden determination.

'Nothing about it that shouldn't be revealed,' he declared. 'It was about Sheila's stories, inspector,' he continued. 'Mr. Darnworth made fun of them — usually choosing a time when company was present in which to do it. He called them rubbish and other things. I suppose he thought it was funny, but I didn't. I told him so many a time, but it didn't have much effect.'

Elaine declared in a loud clear voice: 'I didn't blame dad a bit for showing up Sheila the way he did. Writing thrillers, indeed! Such piffle! Trying to make yourself look smarter than the rest of us, more like it. That was your only reason!'

'That,' Barry Crespin said with quiet restraint, 'is just how Mr. Darnworth used to carry on — and you supported him, Mrs. Darnworth, I'm sorry to say. Family jealousy, I'd call it,'

'I'd rather we dropped the subject,' Sheila said.

'I don't blame you,' Gossage remarked. 'Well, we've made a bit of progress. I knew none of you minded much that Mr. Darnworth had been removed from your midst, but I'm glad to know the reasons — except yours, Miss Darnworth.'

'My reason?' Elaine's bright blue eyes opened wide. 'What on earth reason should I have for disliking my father?'

'It isn't far to seek, inspector,' her mother said, ignoring the angry look Elaine flashed on her. 'Elaine and her father quarrelled continually — not about anything specific but as a matter of course. She is a self-willed girl and he was a grimly determined man, and most of his aims were utterly opposed to those of my daughter. Elaine loves animals; my husband did not. He had social plans for her and she would have none of them. And so on . . . You understand?'

Gossage was nodding slowly and Elaine was silent, going on with her dinner in bitter resentment.

'Yes,' Gossage answered, sighing, 'I think I do. But, all of you, don't think I feel any the less friendly or more unfriendly towards any of you for what you've said. There is nothing unique about the domestic conditions you have described; you come across them in many families. At least I do in the course of my work. One person in the family — usually the head of it — is too overbearing and everybody else is thrown off balance because of it. The same conditions obviously obtained here.'

'Which puts all of us in a bad light,' Sheila said moodily. 'You believe one of us killed my father, don't you, Mr. Gossage?'

'So might lots of other people . . . '

There was silence, and it lasted a full minute.

'You mean . . . outside enemies?' Gregory Bride asked finally.

'Why not? Mr. Darnworth was a financier: outside enemies are by no means an unlikely possibility.' The chief inspector looked serious for a moment, then his red face was suddenly smiling. 'Don't take too much unto yourselves. In fact, suppose we change the subject altogether and talk about — '

Andrews approached the inspector. 'Begging your pardon, sir, but you are wanted on the telephone.'

Gossage went to the telephone in the hall. Craddock was on the line.

'I've had a check up made on Barry Crespin's radio stores,' he said. 'Everything is in older. He has two radio stores and one of his assistants did ring him up at the manor this morning. It was a radio breakdown in a public institution and only he could fix it.'

'I see. Many thanks, Craddock. 'By.'

As he turned from the telephone there was a knock at the front door and Andrews came from the dining-room and admitted a policeman.

'Message for the inspector,' he announced gruffly. 'Private.'

Andrews motioned with his hand and then retired. The constable saluted as Gossage walked across the hall toward him.

‘We’ve finished searching the grounds,’ he reported. ‘No sign of a weapon.’

‘Or footprints either?’

‘Not a trace, sir, I’ll stake my job on it that nobody’s been tramping about these grounds for long enough, and the soil being wet prints’d show quick enough if there were any.’

Gossage nodded slowly and opened the front door wide. There was a full moon rising outside.

‘You’re right, they would,’ he agreed. ‘Well, that’s all, thanks. You’d better report back to headquarters.’

8

For some time after dinner, when the party had retired to the lounge, Mrs. Darnworth sat in her wheelchair, reading, watched over by the taciturn Preston. Louise was seated near her, sewing. Gossage remained silent, his eyes half shut, smoke curling out of his pipe. Sergeant Blair was in any easy chair, smoking cigarettes and glancing through the notes he had made. In a far corner Sheila was at a table, writing. Near her on the divan sprawled Barry Crespin, looking through a radio periodical. The only ones talking were Bride and Elaine. They were arguing about something.

'Oh, for heaven sake be quiet!' Mrs. Darnworth broke in impatiently, turning her head towards them. 'Or if you do talk let it be about something we can all understand. Isn't there enough trouble in the house without you dragging in the fourth dimension?'

'But, Mrs. Darnworth, it is a subject of such pre-eminent scientific interest — ' Gregory Bride spread his hands and looked amazed at the lack of academic intelligence. 'And I still insist — '

'There must be better things to talk about,' Mrs. Darnworth interrupted him.

'To be sure,' Gossage agreed, straightening up. 'For instance, I'd like a little information concerning this house.'

Immediately he became the focal point of interest. Sheila stopped writing. Gregory Bride raised his eyebrows and looked annoyed at the switch in topic. Barry Crespin laid down his radio periodical.

'All of you,' Gossage went on, 'have a distinct advantage over Sergeant Blair and myself in that you know the complete layout of the Manor. Right?'

Everybody nodded, though some so slightly it was barely perceptible.

'What do you wish to know?' Mrs. Darnworth asked.

'Well, as one approaches the manor up the drive there are six upper windows. From left to right — seen from the drive

— I'd like to know what windows they are, to which rooms they belong.'

Sheila said: 'The first on the left, to the left of the porch, is Sergeant Blair's bedroom at present; the next one is yours, inspector. Then comes Mr. Crespin's, mother's, Mr. Bride's, and then the boxroom . . . That makes six.'

Gossage had taken out his notebook and upon a leaf of it drew six squares. In each one, as the girl enumerated, he put the relative identification.

'Thanks,' he said, musing over the result. 'Then the room over Mr. Darnworth's study is occupied by you, Mr. Bride?'

'I?' The young physicist looked surprised. 'Yes, I suppose so. What are you getting at, Inspector?'

'Getting at? Nothing! You have to sleep somewhere!'

'You're a bit wrong though, Mr. Gossage,' Sheila added. 'Both Mr. Bride's bedroom and the boxroom are over the study.'

'I'd like to verify it. Any objection to my seeing your bedroom, Mr. Bride?'

'Of course not. Come on up and I'll show you.'

'And yours, Mrs. Darnworth? And yours, Mr. Crespin?' Gossage got to his feet and looked at them both in turn.

'As you like,' Crespin shrugged, 'though I can assure you it's a perfectly ordinary room.' He rose from the divan and lounged across to the side of Bride. Mrs. Darnworth watched his movements and then half glanced behind her.

'Preston — '

'Yes, mum?'

'Show Mr. Gossage my room. We must not put difficulties in the way of police.'

A look of grim disapproval went over the handyman's thin face, but he obeyed the order and went out of the lounge behind Gregory Bride, Crespin and Gossage. When they reached the head of the stairs Gossage turned to him.

'I'll see Mrs. Darnworth's room first, Preston — then you can get back to her. She may need you.'

'All right. This is it,' he said briefly, and opened the fourth door along the corridor.

'And I'm telling you straight, Mr. Gossage, I don't like all this poking and prying,' he added. 'Y've no call to suspect Mrs. Darnworth of anything. For one thing she can't walk, as y'can see, and she's an honest woman.'

'I'm not suspecting anybody of anything, Preston. All I want to look at is the view from Mrs. Darnworth's bedroom.'

'The view?' Preston repeated suspiciously. 'But it's dark!'

'When I saw a policeman at the front door an hour ago I noticed that the full moon was getting up. It'll do for me.'

Preston looked dubious and stood aside. Bride and Crespin glanced at each other and shrugged away their feelings. Gossage went into the bedroom and looked about him. In general it was identical in furniture with his own, save that there was an invalid table and the general layout was far more feminine. The room itself did not appear to interest him, however. Going to the window he drew back the curtains and cupped his hands round his eyes and against the glass as he stared into the night.

When at last he turned back into the room he was nodding to himself.

'Quite a lovely night,' he commented.

'By the way, Preston, where does the girl Louise sleep? Which is her room?'

Preston nodded to a door across the corridor. 'There. Next to it is Miss Sheila's room, and on the other side is Miss Elaine's.'

'And your room? And Andrews'?'

'In an upstairs wing on the side of the house.' Gossage's pipe crackled for a moment or two as he thought something out. Then he nodded to the doors on the opposite side of the corridor.

'These rooms, then, all face the river?'

'Yes.'

'Miss Sheila's room, Louise's and the others do not face the drive?'

'No. They look out over the conservatories and to the country beyond.'

'I think I might see your room next, Mr. Bride,' Gossage said. 'As for you, Preston, you might as well return to Mrs. Darnworth.'

The handyman nodded silently and went off.

Gregory Bride opened the door next to the end one, motioning inside it. Then he stood, Crespin beside him, watching as Gossage strolled into the room and looked about. Then he went to the window, glanced outside, and then went back to the door.

'These rooms look as though they're standardized,' he said, closing the door quietly behind him. 'Every one alike, the only difference being whether a man or woman is the occupant. Well, that leaves only your room, Mr. Crespin.'

'Come this way,' the radio engineer invited, but when he got to his room and opened the door he frowned. 'Look, inspector, are you looking for something in these rooms? I mean, you know that they all face the drive; you know that they're all more or less like each other.'

Gossage said: 'I'm just getting a mental impression of the layout.'

'I think I'll go back downstairs,' Bride said, turning away. 'I haven't finished convincing Elly that the fourth dimension isn't time.'

'If you ask me, I don't think you ever

will,' Gossage called after him; then he went into Crespin's room. As before, he glanced about him, finally settling in a comfortable chair.

'Have a seat, Mr. Crespin. I'd like a few words with you now we have a quiet moment.'

The radio engineer closed the door and perched himself on the ottoman at the foot of the bed. He held out a gold cigarette case, then as Gossage indicated his pipe he took out a cigarette for himself and lit it.

Gossage waited for a moment, his pipe sizzling, then he said:

'Now let's get a few things clear, Mr. Crespin. I believe you worked until the early hours of yesterday morning on the radio, which led you to get a rest before dinner last evening?'

Crespin nodded his head a look of mild inquiry on his round face. He waited for a moment or two for Gossage to say something further, but he remained contemplating the floor.

'I suppose you find that suspicious?' Barry Crespin asked at length.

'Suspicious?' The chief inspector looked up in surprise. 'Why, no. A man can go to sleep if he wants to, and he can repair a radio if he wants to. I'm simply checking up on the statement of Andrews. He told me that last evening he had strict orders to inform you when it was half-past 7, and that if you were asleep not to disturb you.'

'That's quite right,' Crespin agreed. 'I went out at about 6 for a stroll to try and clear myself up a bit — you know how frowsy you get after missing a night's sleep — but instead the air seemed to make me more tired than ever. I came up to my room here and lay down on the bed. I remember hearing Sheila playing the piano. Then I got into bed properly and must have gone to sleep. I woke at about 10 to 8 and by a last minute scramble managed to get down to dinner on time.'

'You came back in the house again at what time?'

'Just before 7. I was only out for an hour.'

'Can you recall,' Gossage asked slowly,

'if you awakened naturally or did some sound cause it?'

'I think some sound must have caused it. Usually, once asleep, I go on for hours. But I've not the least idea what it could have been.'

Gossage strolled to the window and stood gazing out into the moonlit grounds.

'The problem to me,' Crespin said, coming over to join him in contemplating the view, 'is how anybody ever got in the study to kill Darnworth, with a solid window and the door locked on the inside.'

'I suppose,' Gossage said, 'you've no idea what sort of an invention Mr. Bride was going to show Mr. Darnworth before he was murdered?'

'No. You'll find Greg Bride a bit of a queer stick — Clever, mind you, when it comes to science. Quite a few scientific gadgets on the market are his, financed by Darnworth.'

Barry Crespin grinned ruefully and rubbed his untidy blond head, then the cigarette began bobbing up and down in his mouth as he began talking again.

'Unfortunately I haven't got that brand of brains. I never invented anything in my life.'

'You say that Darnworth financed quite a few of Mr. Bride's inventions? I wonder, then, why it was necessary for Miss Darnworth to become engaged to him in order to push him into her father's good books.'

'Is that what you've been told?' Crespin threw back his head, and laughed silently. 'I'd advise you to discount all that, inspector. Elaine became engaged to Greg for one reason only — because she loves him. She loves his science, his self-assurance, everything about him. But a girl like Elaine won't admit on principle that she's capable of loving a man, so she digs up an excuse.'

'I see,' Gossage said, nodding. 'Then Darnworth and Bride got on all right together?'

'I wouldn't say that. They had plenty of arguments — and maybe they had some rows in the privacy of that study when it came to business deals. Darnworth was a man who enjoyed rubbing everybody the wrong way, including his own flesh and blood. He was an egoist, weighted down with money, supremely confident of himself, and having a profound contempt for women. As I said at dinner, I never liked the way he treated Sheila.'

'Sheila,' Gossage said, 'is a nice girl. Bright and sensitive. Clever, eh?'

'Yes.' Crespin nodded pensively. 'She has one thing Bride has — creative power. Only hers is literary. She's most thorough over her work — believes in realism to the last detail.'

'And she writes thrillers, eh?'

'Murder thrillers chiefly.' Crespin came forward, considering something carefully. 'I don't know if I ought to tell you this,' he said finally, 'but I'll risk it. Did you ever hear of D. J. Harper?'

'Why, yes. Pretty well known murder-mystery writer. I've read some of his books.'

'The 'his' should be 'her',' Crespin corrected. 'To be exact — Sheila.'

9

Gossage showed surprise.

'Then her work has been published? I'd got the idea, from the retiring way she goes about things, that she wrote in secret and then burned the manuscripts. Why the yarns I've read of Harper's — Sheila's — are very slick. Some of the methods used for killing are . . . ' He broke off. 'Why all the secrecy?' he asked.

'I'm telling you this in confidence.' Crespin had a serious face. 'The old man and family in general made such ridicule of her work when she first started, and wounded her pride so much, that she has never told anybody that her work has been accepted. She has an agent and her own bank account under a pen name. Outside of me — and the agent and publishers of course — nobody knows that she is a success. I beg you not to tell her that you know. She'd never forgive me.'

Gossage smiled. 'You can rely on me, Mr. Crespin. Tell me, how long have you known her — or am I too inquisitive?'

'It began when I was in the services, and Sheila was in the services too, you know, just as Elaine was in the land army. I was doing a bit of mountaineering in Switzerland when the war threatened and I came back to join up. While abroad I met Sheila, but it was only a brief meeting with nothing serious about it, and then before I even had a chance to know her second name circumstances separated us. After the war she saw my radio advertisement in a newspaper. She knew my full name and sent for me to come and do a repair here. That was six months ago. Our friendship deepened and . . . ' Crespin shrugged. 'That's how it was. Now we're engaged . . . '

'Sheila has a good deal of faith in you,' Gossage said. 'She believes you can do anything you want.'

'That's a tall order, Mr. Gossage, but I do my best. I want to own a whole chain of radio stores. I want to extend my business as far as possible. I'm crazy about radio.'

'But not so crazy as to desert the faithful old portable gramophone, I see,' Gossage commented, nodding under the dressing table.

Crespin looked and then smiled. 'Oh that! It's an old portable I carry around with me, fitted with a repeater gadget. You know — plays the same record twice over at one winding. I'm a swing fan. I've got half a dozen records that I take everywhere with me.'

He went to the wardrobe and pulled out a golf bag full of clubs and six 10-inch records, all boogie-woogie music, so he said. He returned them very carefully to the wardrobe floor and closed the door again.

The chief inspector contemplated the golf bag in the corner for a moment, then he said: 'Well, maybe we'd better be getting back downstairs. Thanks for the revelations, Mr. Crespin. And they'll be safe enough with me.'

In the lounge, Gossage strolled over to where Sergeant Blair was tracing meaningless designs on a leaf of his notebook. The inspector said: 'I'm going to take another look round the study. Come on.'

Blair jumped up promptly.

Inside the study with the lights switched on Gossage locked the door.

'Good,' he observed, relaxing. 'This is better. I'm one of those modest coves who can never work while somebody is watching me.'

He sat down in the swivel chair and studied the desk in front of him. Switching on the desk light he watched the sudden flood of brilliance that made the light of the twin-globed electrolier seem superfluous.

'A reconstruction, sir?' Blair asked, coming forward.

Gossage did not respond immediately. He was frowning at three small notches, obviously new, in the edge of the desk, just as if a sharp blade had hacked there.

He said: 'I'm Darnworth, and here' — tapping the back of his head — 'is where the bullet has hit me. It comes from above. What do you see?'

Sergeant Blair stooped so as to be at eye level with the back of Gossage's head and looked above him. In his opinion this was simply going over old ground. There was only the paneled oak ceiling — solid, impregnably solid — and 10 feet away the electrolier with its rosette flush with the ceiling.

'There's nothing, sir,' he said.

'There's got to be!' Gossage said. 'We've stuck at a brick wall long enough. Somehow Darnworth was shot from above and we don't leave here until we find out how.'

'Suppose,' Blair asked, 'he was shot outside the study somewhere and then brought in here?'

'That only leaves us in the same mess,' Gossage growled. 'How did the killer get out and leave the door locked on the inside? And the key in the lock at that! Besides, Darnworth always spent the hour from 7 to 8 in here. Why then should he be killed outside? It was in here all right, Harry, and it has a logical explanation. If we don't want the A.C. jumping down our throats we've got to find out what that explanation is.' He glanced about the study and then nodded to the bell-push. 'Give it a jab, will you?'

Blair obliged and then went over to unlock the door. After a while Andrews appeared, as silent and half bent in the middle as usual.

'Sir?'

'I'd like a stepladder, Andrews,' Gossage said, swinging round in the swivel chair to face him. 'The tallest you have.'

'Yes, sir — right away.'

Just for a moment a change of expression crossed Andrews' face. Perhaps it was puzzlement, perhaps suspicion. It was not easy to tell. In any event, he added nothing further, but brought the stepladder.

Setting the ladder about a foot from the electrolier the inspector climbed to the step next to the top and looked about him.

'Nothing unusual up there, sir, is there?' Blair asked.

'With the deepest regret I answer no.' Gossage peered at the paneling intently in all directions. 'There isn't a hole big enough for a worm to get through, never mind a gun.'

He turned and looked at the electrolier, shading his eyes.

'Switch these darned lights off,' he grumbled.

Blair pushed the switch and the only light then came from the desk light.

'Solid — as — a — rock,' Gossage said, pulling at the copper tube jutting from the ceiling. 'The rosette at the top holds it flush and level with the panels. I can't shift it one way or the other. Pity. I had an idea that somehow . . .'

He stopped, sat down on top of the steps and drew hard at his pipe. For several minutes he sat thinking. Then he stood up again and for a second time went over the electrolier circumspectly, examining the rosette at the top of the tube flush with the panels, then the second rosette at the bottom of the tube. It was of smaller and of different pattern and color to the one at the top. About an inch above it were the bases of the two semi-circular tubes that at their ends carried the now extinguished electric bulbs.

'I don't see how the electrolier can have had anything to do with it, sir,' Blair remarked. 'It's obviously a fixture — '

'Not entirely,' Gossage interrupted him, peering at the top rosette again. 'This top rosette isn't screwed into the ceiling. That means the whole fixture must be held in place somewhere above.'

'Even so,' Blair persisted, 'the desk is 10 feet away from the electrolier. That is what you're supposing, sir, isn't it?'

'And at the bottom of this tube, where this lower rosette is, there's a screw thread and nothing screwed on to it. Hmmm . . .'

Gossage came down the steps and stood pondering when he got to the bottom.

He said: 'Most electroliers are screwed into the ceiling and this one isn't. And that screw thread is very odd, too. I'd like a close look at the spot where this electrolier is fastened. Come with me.'

He locked the study door on the outside and walked to the lounge.

Sheila and Crespin, and Bride and Elaine were still there.

'Been on the prowl, Mr. Gossage?' Sheila inquired.

He nodded. 'A habit I have, Miss Sheila. Tell me, does the top of the study electrolier connect to the boxroom or Mr. Bride's bedroom?'

'Connect to it?' Sheila repeated vaguely. 'How — how do you mean?'

'He means,' Barry Crespin said, 'that the electrolier in the study must connect to the floor of either the boxroom or Greg's room — or just under the floor, rather. Which room is it?'

'I don't know,' Sheila replied, shaking her head. 'I've never bothered to find out about such things.'

'Perhaps Andrews will know,' the inspector said, and rang for the butler.

Andrews said the connection was with the boxroom. 'I remember that a couple of years ago we had some trouble with that light,' he said. 'There are three loose boards in the floor of the boxroom near the wall — the same wall which belongs to Mr. Bride's bedroom.'

'And who has the key to the boxroom? You?'

'No, sir. Mrs. Darnworth.'

'Is there something valuable in that room?'

'I haven't the slightest idea, sir. All I know is that the mistress has the only key, and I would suggest that you apply to her for it, as the police had to do last night when they searched the house.'

Gossage looked at Elaine.

'Where is your mother, Miss Darnworth?' he asked.

'Probably getting ready for bed. She retires early every evening. She went upstairs a moment or two before you came back in here.'

Gossage jerked his head at Blair and they went up the stairs.

'Queerest household I've struck in some time, sir,' Blair confided. ''Do you think that perhaps the boxroom contains a family skeleton?'

'How should I know? It's common sense to suppose, though, that is isn't just an ordinary boxroom if the old girl herself hangs on to the key. We'll — '

At the end of the softly lighted corridor Preston was kneeling beside the wheelchair Mrs. Darnworth had been using that evening. He was apparently oiling the wheels.

'Just the chap I want,' Gossage said.

'What's the matter?' Preston asked shortly.

'I want a word with Mrs. Darnworth,' Gossage said.

Preston got up with deliberate movements and stood looking at Gossage with dark distrust. 'Y'haven't got the decency to let a weary lady alone, have y'?' he demanded bitterly. 'You have to go prying and snoopin' and upsetting everybody just to satisfy some crazy theory y've got, I suppose. Well, I'll tell y'this. Mr. Nosey Parker Gossage, you're not seeing her. Not until tomorrow. See?'

'This,' Gossage answered, smiling, 'won't wait until tomorrow.'

10

Preston looked sour. 'Y'don't have to be funny with me! I don't trust you, or your kind, and as long as I'm paid to look after Mrs. Darnworth's interests I'll do it. She means a lot t'me does the old lady. Now let me get on with my work. She'll be wantin' this chair in her room tomorrow — well oiled.'

'I've little doubt of it, Preston, but I still mean to see her.' Gossage patted his thin arm encouragingly. 'Come on, man, don't let your loyalty turn you into a nuisance.'

Preston snatched his arm away, glowering.

'Keep y'hands off me, inspector! I don't like that sort o' thing! And I'd advise y'to get back downstairs — An' stay' there, what's more! Whatever it is y'want can wait until the morning.'

'It can, can it?' Blair broke in angrily. 'And I've had enough of this, sir,' he added, striding forward to Mrs. Darnworth's bedroom door.

'Wait!' Gossage raised a hand. 'Wait a minute, Harry. I'll take care of this.' He turned back to the set-faced handyman.

'I don't need to see Mrs. Darnworth,' the inspector said. 'All I want is the key to the boxroom.'

'Why?' Preston snapped.

'That's my business, Preston. And I'd suggest,' Gossage added, hard edges coming to his voice, 'that you stop making yourself infernally awkward!'

'I've a duty to do, Mr. Inspector, an' I'm doing it. That duty is to see that Mrs. Darnworth isn't disturbed until tomorrow morning — that is once Louise has put her to bed.'

'Louise is in there, then?' Gossage asked. 'Then Mrs. Darnworth is still awake?'

He waited no longer but knocked sharply on the door. Preston stood in morose silence, his mouth a hard, set line and the malevolent glitter still in his eyes.

The bedroom door opened silently perhaps three inches and the pale, blue-nosed face of Louise appeared.

'Yes?' she whispered. 'What do you want? Oh, it's you, Mr. Gossage! Is something wrong?'

'I don't wish to disturb Mrs. Darnworth,' Gossage said, 'but would you kindly ask her it I might have the key to the boxroom?'

'The key to — to the boxroom?' Louise was surprised. 'But — what for?'

Gossage compressed his lips. This was becoming irksome —

'Louise! Louise!' It was Mrs. Darnworth's sharp, commanding voice, from inside the room. 'Ask Mr. Gossage to come in. I'd like a word with him.'

The girl glanced quickly behind her.

'Yes, Mrs. Darnworth,' she said, and opened the door wide enough for Gossage to enter, then closed it again behind her. His eyes moved to where Mrs. Darnworth lay in bed, propped up with pillows, a book under the reading lamp at her side.

'I had no wish to intrude, madam,' Gossage apologized.

'I'm sure you hadn't — but I overheard

your request.' The cold blue eyes glanced at Louise. 'That will be all for tonight, Louise,' Mrs. Darnworth said. 'I'll ring if I need you.'

Louise left the room quickly and Gossage stood looking down on Jessica Darnworth.

'So you want the key to the boxroom, Inspector?' she said. 'Why? Something to do with your investigation?'

'At this juncture I hardly know. I merely wish to satisfy myself as to how the study electrolier is fixed.'

She measured him, smiling tautly. 'The electrolier? But you surely don't think the shot which killed my husband came from that, do you?'

'All I want is the key,' Gossage replied. 'I believe Divisional Inspector Craddock asked you for it last night?'

'He did, and I had Preston watch what went on while those men prowled about the boxroom.'

Gossage hesitated on a question but did not ask it.

'Very well,' Mrs. Darnworth said finally, 'you shall have the key. Would you mind handing me that bag?'

He picked it up, a small expensive handbag, from the bedside table and gave it to her. She took a fairly large and definitely old-fashioned key from a center pocket.

'I'm letting you have this, Mr. Gossage,' she said, 'for one reason only — because I want to help you find my husband's murderer, as I told you earlier on today. I am satisfied that you will confine yourself purely to investigation and will not go beyond it, any more than the police did last night.'

Gossage smiled coldly. 'I am sorry, Mrs. Darnworth, but I cannot guarantee to limit my curiosity. I might even turn the boxroom inside out.'

She hesitated for a long moment, then with the slightest of nods handed the key over.

'You are a man of the world, Mr. Gossage,' she said, and he could see the hard shell cracking and something of the real Jessica Darnworth emerging from behind it. 'I like your frank approach, your easy geniality with us all despite a great deal of provocation — particularly from my elder daughter. I want you to understand that I really do want to help you find the murderer of my husband. Not because I had any regard for him: I hadn't, not one jot! But because murder must be punished.'

'Thank you.' Gossage's voice was unaccustomedly reserved. 'For your promise of co-operation, I mean.'

'I don't know who killed him,' she went on fiercely. 'But I feel sure it was somebody in this house. We all hated him. He was overbearing, cruel, derisive. I am sure you will find the killer. Don't spare him — or her.'

When Gossage stepped out to the corridor, Preston was not there. He had gone downstairs, Blair said.

The door of the boxroom opened stiffly, and Blair felt inside for the light switch and snapped it on. Nothing happened.

'No bulb.' he muttered. 'I have a flashlight in my room, sir. Be back in a minute.'

Gossage nodded and stood just inside

the doorway, waiting, the smell of dust strong in his nostrils.

Blair came hurrying back, and flashed the light beam into the boxroom. It settled on tin deed boxes, old trunks, part of an old bedstead, a section of what had once been a wardrobe, and a small table minus one of its legs.

'Junk!' Blair growled.

Gossage took a few steps into the room and paused, frowning.

'That's odd,' he said. 'Years of dust on the trunks and other stuff, and yet none on the floor, at least not where it's uncovered.'

Blair considered the fact.

'Probably Craddock's men brushed the floor, sir —'

'What for? They could see if anything were on the floor, dust or no dust. And evidently they didn't look in these trunks and deed boxes for the reason that the undisturbed dust on them shows they haven't been tampered with.'

'I have heard of criminals adding dust after crime sir,' Sergeant Blair murmured.

'And I've heard of the moon being

made of green cheese — but I don't have to credit it. The point here, Harry, is that somebody else has been in this room either before or after the police and moved the dust — to prevent any footprints being traced.'

'Then it must have been before, sir,' Blair said, 'otherwise Craddock and his boys would have seen the prints.'

'Right.'

Gossage went forward again, casting the flashlight beam along the bases of the trunks and boxes. Then he pointed.

'I was right. Look! The dust is piled up in ridges round these edges. Somebody's brushed it aside.'

They looked at the small plain glass window. It was of the sash variety and locked. Blair turned.

'We came to look at the electrolier support, didn't we, sir?'

Gossage nodded and they moved to the wall on their right, the one dividing them from Gregory Bride's bedroom. Immediately the beam fell on the spot they wanted. Three of the floorboards had been sawn through, making a movable square of about 18 inches. Without the least effort Blair pried them up with his penknife blade.

In the cavity that had been there was a loose piece of steel chain, about eight inches long, made up of six strong links. Through the seventh link from the loose end a narrow iron bar was fixed horizontally over a wide, cast-iron cylinder which itself was secured to the top side of the paneled ceiling by a series of screws, corroded with age.

Twining loosely from the open end of the electrolier's central tube, and then snaking between the links of the chain, was a double wire finishing in twin plugs which were pegged into two sockets fixed in the floor beam. To these sockets ran the house wiring.

'Everything in order, sir,' Blair said. 'The electrolier is held by the chain, which is fastened to this hook on the inside of the rosette which is flush with the paneled ceiling below. The bar through the links holds it taut — hence no screws are needed in the ceiling — and the bar is supported by this metal cylinder that is screwed to the topside of the panel. Then the wires plug in the sockets. The electrolier can be lowered simply by unplugging the sockets and putting a rope through the chain. The cylinder is wide enough to take the two plugs as you lower.'

Gossage said nothing. He was on his knees, the flashlight beam blazing into the cavity.

'This hook is bent back,' he said presently. 'This one, I mean, to which the chain is fastened. And sharply back, too. For some reason the top has been bent away from the normal central position. And — what's the idea of this smaller tube, I wonder?'

For the moment Blair did not quite see what his superior meant, but when he did he peered into the cavity more earnestly. He observed the bent hook just like a backwardly tilted '?', then he saw something else.

At first sight it looked as if the two electric wires came out of the top of a single tube — the main electrolier tube — but now it was evident they came up the sides of a second tube, of smaller diameter, in the middle of the big tube.

The smaller one was, in turn, clipped on to the edge of the large one by spring clamps, similar to those on a fountain-pen cap.

'I'll wager my shirt and next year's rose bushes that this second tube doesn't need to be here!' Gossage said.

He reached into the cavity and tried to seize the inner tube, but the space was too narrow for his fingers and thumb to get a grip.

'Get the pliers out of my bag,' he ordered.

Blair brought the pliers from Gossage's 'murder bag', and the chief inspector took them from him.

'We can't pull this inner tube up,' he said, after some minutes of effort, 'and it's probably because that rosette the bottom is holding it. In that case, I'll take a risk — ' And the steel jaws of the pliers began to work the spring clips back and forth. After a moment or two one of them snapped, then the other followed it.

Tense-faced both men watched the

inner tube slide downward and from below there came a muffled bump.

'It's gone,' Blair whispered. 'Dropped right out of the bottom of the main tube and hit the study carpet below. In fact, I can see it.' he added, peering through the electrolier tube. 'Yes, the desk light is still on, giving a glow along the floor. I can see a bit of the stepladder, too. Take a look.'

Gossage did so and saw a tiny circle of study carpet with the edge of the steps and part of the fallen tube just within the area.

'Definitely we are getting warmer,' he said grimly. 'But there's huge chunks of the problem left unsolved. We — '

'What,' Blair interrupted him, musing, 'do you make of that, sir?'

He was pointing to the boards at the edge of the cavity. For three-quarters of the way along its length, at right angles to it, somebody had drawn five thick straight pencil lines. One of them, the centermost, had a line at right angles to it on its tip, making it a horizontal T.

11

Gossage studied the lines with his brows down. Then at last he shook his head slowly.

'I don't know,' he said frankly. 'This has got to be thought out. Put the boards back and we'll go down to the study and have a look at that tube.'

They hurried downstairs together and re-entered the study, Blair locking the door behind them. He turned to the center of the room again to find Gossage had picked up the tube and taken it over to the desk where he was examining it under the light.

'By all that's neat and ingenious,' he muttered at length. 'Take a look at this, Harry.'

Sergeant Blair watched, then his eyebrows went up as, cupping the copper rosette in his palm, Gossage squeezed it. It folded up flat like the ribs on a closing umbrella, the 'leaves' of the rosette lying parallel with the tube itself.

'It's simple enough, sir.' Blair ventured a modest smile. 'I'm a bit of an amateur magician; do a turn for the kids at Christmas and so on. This rosette is a variation of two magical tricks, the one known as the 'magic cabbage' and the other as, I think, the 'umbrella problem'.'

Gossage grinned and laid the tube on the blotter. He sat down in the swivel chair and began to refill his pipe. 'Go on, Harry,' he urged.

'It's like this. The 'magic cabbage' is an affair of silks and wires made to resemble a cabbage, small enough to fit in the palm of the hand. It lies flat when folded up. Release it, and you have what looks like an impossibly large cabbage from an impossibly small space.

'The umbrella trick is different, and there's no point in my going through the whole routine, even granting I could remember it. In principle, you have eight ribs all flat to the umbrella shaft, as in an ordinary umbrella. You shoot it through a tube that has apparently been empty, and once the flat umbrella gets beyond the tube, the springs work and the ribs open out. The trick relies for effect on the principle that you can't pull an open umbrella through a narrow tube.'

Gossage sat smoking, his eyes on the rosette.

'In that case, then, somebody made an artificial rosette of copper with each leaf springed and fastened it on a tube narrower than the tube of the electrolier itself. Then he, or she, pushed the tube in the bigger tube from the top, the rosette lying flat as it went down the tube. When it reached the bottom it sprang open, and the tube could not be drawn back again. The clips stopped it from falling out.'

'That seems about it, sir. The whole thing could be worked from above. As we saw for ourselves, the electrolier tube is amply wide enough to admit of this smaller tube without the twin cords getting in the way. And they branch off into those two right-angled arms before reaching bottom, so that a clear passage is left for the smaller 'rosette tube'.'

Gossage examined the rosette again, wagging his head over its neatness. It was quite obvious now that the copper was different from the rest of the electrolier.

'This,' he said, 'enables us to get the picture a little more in focus. We know that there is a screw-thread which doesn't seem to serve any useful purpose, on the base of the electrolier there.' He turned to look at it. 'That, doubtless, is where the real rosette was originally screwed. Clearly, then, the murderer, after having mode all arrangements, unscrewed the real rosette and left a clear hole in the bottom of the electrolier tube.

'Would Darnworth notice it? Not a chance in ten million. Do you look at the electric light fittings in your home when, as far as you know, they haven't changed ever since you came into the place? Of course you don't. The murderer was right in his assumption that there was nothing to fear from that quarter. Then afterwards, when the murder had been committed, knowing the police would investigate, he — or it may be she — covered up tracks by pushing this false rosette down the tube from above. The rosette sprang into place, the tube was clipped, and a casual look at the electrolier by the police would reveal nothing unusual. An open-end tube would have drawn suspicion, which the false rosette counterbalanced. Obviously the killer knew it would not be possible to put the real rosette back.'

There was a long silence in the study. Gossage blew a cloud of smoke at the desk lamp, and Sergeant Blair looked up at the electrolier speculatively. Finally he gave his thoughts words.

'We can't help ourselves being drawn to the conclusion that the electrolier is the source of the tragedy, sir — but how could it be? We can look down the tube, but it only shows the carpet immediately underneath it. Darnworth was where you're seated, about 10 feet away. Assuming the electrolier could be tilted to be in line with him, two big factors come up for consideration: the electrolier couldn't be moved because its rosette is flush with the ceiling, and even if it could, it couldn't be swung out of the perpendicular from above.'

Sergeant Blair stopped wading through

the morass and shrugged his shoulders.

'I'm stuck for the moment. I'm afraid. Maybe something will occur to me later on.'

Gossage didn't answer. He was thinking so deeply that his pipe had gone out. His eyes were fixed on the tube and rosette, and there was about him the still detachment of concentration. At length he relaxed and took his pipe from his teeth, grinning faintly.

'I'm going to let it simmer,' he decided. 'There is an answer. Tomorrow I'll go for a long ramble and probably get that answer. Nothing like walking to get your brain working.'

Chief Inspector Gossage had the enviable gift of being able to draw down the blinds round his mind as a shopkeeper does over his wares. He was asleep within 10 minutes of getting to bed, not one vestige of the problem remaining to form the nucleus of a distorted dream.

The next day was Sunday, and when he arrived at breakfast he found all save Mrs. Darnworth had assembled. The two younger women looked vaguely curious;

the two men entirely indifferent. Sergeant Blair seemed worried.

Several times Elaine tried machine-gun tactics to pierce Gossage's armor, and failed. Sheila tried too, by less forceful methods and also came to grief. Gossage had reached the stage where he absorbed everything and gave nothing away. Then the moment breakfast was over he made tracks for Mrs. Darnworth's bedroom, Blair hurrying behind him.

'Right you are, sir.'

Louise admitted Gossage into Mrs. Darnworth's bedroom. He found her with pillows at her back with breakfast on a tray across her knees. In a corner nearby was the oiled wheelchair.

'Good morning, inspector,' she greeted him. 'I trust you are finding everything quite comfortable?'

'Generally speaking, yes.' His red face beamed down on her. 'In other directions, though. I'm a little puzzled — and that's why I'm here. Can you tell me how long it is since anybody entered the boxroom?'

'The police entered on the night my husband — '

'Yes, yes, I know — but I mean before that.'

Jessica Darnworth reflected. 'Oh, it must be two years ago when an electrician came to fix the lighting system.'

'I see. And you have had the key in your possession all that time?'

'Yes. Do you consider that fact — 'significant'?'

'Not particularly; I am simply posing a question. How is the room ever cleaned out?'

'It is never cleaned out — now,' Mrs. Darnworth said. 'Before I had my accident I used to do it myself. I would never allow the staff to do it, but now that is manifestly impossible. So it just isn't done.'

'Do you always keep the boxroom key in your handbag?'

'Or do you mean do I leave it in my handbag so anybody could take a duplicate impression?' Her eyebrows rose in question.

'Yes,' Gossage said. 'That's just what I mean.'

'I'm afraid that would hardly be possible,' she said, reflecting. 'I sleep heavily — drugs, you see — but my door is locked on the outside. Louise has the key. Once I have retired, my daughters never bother me.'

Gossage turned slightly and looked at Louise. She was doing something at the wardrobe, and though her pale ears were hidden under her mousy hair, Gossage guessed that they were probably sticking out a mile.

'Let me try something else, Mrs. Darnworth,' he said finally. 'On the night your husband was murdered — between 7 and 8 — you were in here, I believe? Dressing for dinner?'

'That is so. I had spent all afternoon in bed. Louise was helping me dress.'

'And Preston, I understand, was in the corridor outside waiting to be called to help you downstairs?'

'To carry me downstairs, Inspector. You needn't spare my feelings.'

He shrugged. 'During that period can

you remember if you heard anything outside? I imagine there would be very little noise in here, which should have made outside sounds quite noticeable.'

'Sounds outside?' Her eyes sharpened at him. 'What kind of sounds?'

'Oh, say, the bang of a ladder against the side of the house?'

'No, I didn't hear anything.'

'Did you, Louise?' Gossage looked across at her.

'I didn't hear anything, sir.' Her head shook emphatically.

'All right,' the chief Inspector said. 'I won't bother you any further now, Mrs. Darnworth — or you, Louise — but I'll keep the boxroom key a little longer, if I may?'

'As long as it does not leave your possession you may keep it as long as you wish, inspector'

With a nod Gossage left the room. He shut the door slowly and stood rubbing his head for a moment, then Blair came over to him from further down the corridor.

'Anything new, sir?'

‘No. Harry, nothing new. But I think there’s something queer in that boxroom which we haven’t yet unearthed. Until the time of her accident Mrs. Darnworth always cleaned it out herself. Then after her mishap she locked it up and won’t let anybody else go in. The only person who has been in — bar Craddock and his men — was an electrician two years ago. And that, according to her, is the only time. He we can discount, of course. I’ll wager she watched over him from her wheelchair or had Preston do it.’

‘But there’s nothing but junk in there,’ Blair protested. ‘At least as far as we could tell last night. Might look different now it’s daylight. We could have a look,’ he suggested, with a slight movement towards it.

Gossage shook his head.

‘Not for me, Harry. I might run into more problems and I just don’t want ’em until I’ve got the existing ones straightened out. No, I’m going for a long ramble and chew this thing over, and I’ll also have a word with Craddock. Maybe I’ll come back with something worth having.

And you'd better take charge of this.' He handed over the boxroom key. 'See you later.'

'Yes, sir,' Blair said. Then he brightened as he watched Gossage go down the stairs. After all, the chief had not told him to stop investigating on his own account.

12

The fine November day was closing down in ochre and vermilion sunset as, toward half past 5, 'Crimson Rambler' Gossage entered the last stage of his journey home. He was singing 'Danny Boy' to himself in a pleasing bass and was at peace with all the world.

His long walk, and a chat with Craddock over lunch in Godalming, had cleared up a lot of outstanding problems in his mind. He knew now what he hadn't known before — how Warner Darnworth had been shot, and even more important, the reason for the pencil marks on the boxroom floor. Of course the pencil marks had to be there, especially the one like a horizontal 'T,' otherwise the thing didn't make sense.

As he re-entered Bexley village high street, the four lamps that illuminated it had just been lit.

Thirty yards ahead of him was a large

shining black car, striking an incongruously modern note in the rural scene. The chauffeur had got out and the inspector recognized him as Preston, in dark blue livery.

Silently Gossage moved to one side and took up a position in the doorway of a shop. As it was Sunday, the shop lights were off and hardly anybody was about. Not that he expected anything unusual, but he took the activities of the Darnworth family as part of his curriculum. Anything they did was worth observing.

Perhaps 10 minutes passed, then to his astonishment a small figure in black, a veil covering her face, emerged from one of the small thatched-roof cottages farther up the street. With a slow, deliberate movement she walked to the car and Preston saluted deferentially as he opened the car's rear door.

'Mrs. Darnworth, as I live and breathe!' Gossage muttered to himself. Jessica Darnworth — walking.

The car moved away, and Gossage resumed his walk through the village, glancing at the cottage Mrs. Darnworth had left. Although it had a thatched roof it was better than the average type of cottage dwelling, cleanly whitewashed outside and with a newly painted green front door. Otherwise there was nothing that could give him a clue.

The chief inspector had hardly entered the hall before Sergeant Blair emerged from the lounge with an air of suppressed eagerness. Seeing Elaine and Gregory Bride were also present he bottled up whatever was in his mind and turned to the staircase, where he stood waiting for Gossage as he ascended en route for his bedroom.

'Glad you're back, sir,' he breathed. 'I've got something to tell you.'

'You have, eh? Good enough.' They went to the chief inspector's bedroom and Blair said:

'While you were away, sir, I took it upon myself to have another look through the boxroom — thoroughly and completely.'

'I sort of guessed you might,' Gossage murmured. 'What did you dig out?'

'I didn't actually dig anything out. I left it where it was. Thought it might be safest. I opened the deed boxes and trunks with a master key.'

'You had no right, Harry. I never gave you any such instructions.'

'Neither did you say that I shouldn't. And I think you guessed that I'd do just that, and let me do it so that you'd be able to find out something without overstepping your own authority.'

'There are times when I see a gleam of the psychologist in you,' Gossage said. 'What did you discover?'

'Three things that don't make sense, as far as I can see. In one deed box was a bundle of letters, decidedly lovey-dovey, written by someone named Clinton to Jessica Trant. Obviously the old girl herself before she got married. They're dated over 30 years ago and all postmarked Bexley. Be about a dozen of them. Clinton was certainly crazy about our Jessie.'

'That's interesting, though not unexpected. She said at dinner yesterday that she should have married Clinton Brown instead of Warner Darnworth. Love letters, eh? Secret number one emerges from boxroom. Anything else?'

'Yes, sir. In a second deed box I found a black leather case about six inches long by two wide, lined with scarlet satin. In it are six blonde curls and a small note which said, 'Darling Sheila, two years old.' In a similar case were six dark curls and a similar note saying, 'Darling Elaine, two years old.'

'And there are bundles of manuscript, handwritten and much corrected, and also a couple of pages of the letters of the alphabet executed in a child's hand. I read some parts of the manuscripts and they're thrillers. Pretty good, too. No doubt Sheila wrote 'em.'

'And these were with the curl cases?' Gossage asked.

'Yes, sir, none of which I can understand. It seems pretty clear that Mrs. Darnworth knows exactly what is in the boxroom and yet, according to Sheila and everybody else, she is utterly contemptuous of Sheila's literary efforts, and even of the girl herself. Yet there are those manuscripts of hers, carefully preserved. Why?'

'Why, indeed?' Gossage murmured, returning into the bedroom. 'And that was all you found? No sign of an air rifle?'

Blair shook his head. 'Nothing like that.'

Gossage said: 'I had a word with Craddock, and the boxroom floor was clear of dust when they entered. They didn't examine the trunks and boxes because, as I'd surmised, the dust on them was sufficient guarantee that they hadn't been disturbed. They looked behind them, though, and found no traces of the weapon. They also looked under the floor where the electrolier cavity is but found nothing. They saw nothing significant about the electrolier fittings. So it's obvious that somebody did clean up the floor dust before the police got there — and it's also obvious that it was done to remove all footprint traces.'

'Did the inspector notice those pencil marks?' Blair asked.

'He didn't refer to them, and I

certainly didn't.' Gossage turned to the mirror and adjusted his tie. 'And now, Harry, you'd better hang on to your eyebrows. I've found out that Mrs. Darnworth can walk — as well as you or I.'

'She can what?'

Gossage repeated the statement and briefly added the details of his experience in the village.

'Holy mackerel!' Blair said woefully. 'That certainly does shift the center of gravity. If she can walk she could have gone into the boxroom and then back into her own room and nobody would be any the wiser.'

'That's certainly a possibility,' Gossage admitted. 'But if we are to believe the stories we've been told up to now, somebody would have been the wiser — and I mean Preston: he was waiting in the corridor.'

Suddenly Sergeant Blair snapped his fingers.

'I think I have it, sir! Mrs. Darnworth did it, and Preston knows she did, which is one reason why he's so damned unpleasant to us and so loyal to her. He means to protect her and her phony paralysis secret at all costs. Either that or else Preston did the trick at Mrs. Darnworth's behest . . . On the other hand, Mrs. Darnworth has seemed anxious to help us in the belief that her very frankness would throw us off the track.'

'Mmm . . . ' Gossage said, and didn't look convinced.

'Is there anything wrong with that theory, sir?'

'On the face of it, no. I suppose anything's possible.'

Blair said: 'I tackled Preston about the ladders and he tells me — in fact showed me after some prompting — that they're kept in a shed. There is a set of three extension ladders. Not only are the ladders themselves padlocked together but the shed is locked, and Preston has the key.'

'Has he, by gosh?' Gossage murmured. 'Well, Harry, you've missed one person out of the reckoning — Louise. She knows where the boxroom key is.'

'She wouldn't do it, sir; hasn't got the nerve.'

'Well — anyway. I have at least worked out how the shot was fired and the meaning of the pencil marks, and I believe I know how Warner Darnworth was killed. But I —'

He paused as there were sounds in the corridor. Since he had been on the verge of a revelation Blair looked disappointed. Silently Gossage moved to the bedroom door and opened it. It was Preston, who had come upstairs and taken up a position a little distance along the corridor, leaning against the wall. He was still in his chauffeur's uniform.

Gossage went into the corridor and approached him.

'You here for your usual evening sentry duty, Preston?'

'I am,' he answered coldly.

'Mrs. Darnworth in her room?' Gossage continued, and the man nodded.

'I want a word with her,' Gossage said. 'And with you. Come along.'

For just a moment there was a defiant gleam in Preston's eyes, but he followed

Gossage to Mrs. Darnworth's bedroom door. Blair remained in the doorway of the chief inspector's bedroom.

As usual Louise opened Mrs. Darnworth's bedroom door — a few inches.

'I'd like to see Mrs. Darnworth,' Gossage told her. 'It's most important.'

Mrs. Darnworth's voice declared emphatically, 'Come in, inspector.'

Gossage jerked his head to Preston and entered. The handyman stood by the door with a stern, unyielding face and Gossage went forward slowly. Mrs. Darnworth was seated at the dressing table, dressed as ever in black. She was tidying her hair. When she caught sight of Preston in the mirror's reflection she frowned and turned.

'What are you doing here, Preston? I didn't send for you.'

'I sent for him,' Gossage said. 'This is confidential, Mrs. Darnworth.' His eyes went to Louise.

With a movement of her hand Mrs. Darnworth dismissed the companion, and Gossage was satisfied that with Blair watching the corridor, the girl would not attempt to listen at the keyhole.

'Now, inspector?' The harsh little lines were back around Mrs. Darnworth's jaw and her eyes were sharp.

'Why do you pose as a paralytic, Mrs. Darnworth?'

The question came in Gossage's best straight-to-the-shoulder fashion.

'I beg your pardon?' she asked.

'This afternoon, madam. I saw you walking to your car from a cottage in Bexley.'

Cold acidity was in Mrs. Darnworth's voice. 'I haven't the least idea what you are talking about, Inspector. As for your doubts as to my disability, perhaps you'd care to see the medical reports? Each one ends with 'prognosis negative.' Incurable.'

'You deny that you are able to walk as easily as I?' Gossage snapped.

'Emphatically. And I'd be obliged if you would leave this room, Mr. Gossage.'

He nodded. 'Very well. Later on I shall have to call at the cottage in the village where you visited this afternoon. I'll hazard a guess that I'll find Clinton Drew inside it. I'm prepared to leave everything in abeyance until tomorrow in the hope that by then you'll have decided to tell me the truth yourself.'

He turned to the door and then looked back, his face grim.

'You've been most co-operative so far, Mrs. Darnworth. Why spoil it now?'

13

After dinner Gossage and Blair retired to the study.

Blair leaned forward and became nearly inaudible.

'While you were in the bedroom blowing things up with Mrs. Darnworth, did you ask her about my findings in the boxroom?'

'No I didn't, chiefly because I gave my word that unless necessity demanded it I wouldn't go that far. If the need arises I'll question her quickly enough. Anyway, forget that side for the moment. Let's see if I'm right in my guess at the way Darnworth was killed. We know that the tube of the electrolier, once the rosette is taken away, is hollow, that the two flex wires lie flat at its sides because they are pulled through the right-angled arms near the bottom of the tube. In other words, there is a clear passage through the center tube enabling us to see this study carpet here from above.'

'Right, sir,' Blair agreed.

'As it is now,' the chief inspector went on, 'with the top rosette flush with the paneled ceiling, the electrolier cannot be moved from the perpendicular. But what happens if it is lowered by say two or three links of the chain?'

Blair looked up at it.

'Then it would be possible to swing it out of the perpendicular, but I don't see how that would be possible without something to do it with.'

'The metal cylinder across which the chain-bar is placed is four times as wide as the tube — in fact nearly as wide as the rosette,' Gossage continued. 'Let us assume that we have lowered the electrolier by three links, leaving a space of two inches between top rosette and ceiling, which would never be noticed from down on the floor here. Then what do we do to get leverage? We put a stick into the tube and push the stick in the opposite direction to which we want the electrolier to move. Push left and the electrolier rises to the right — en bloc, the fulcrum being where the bar goes through the chain. The supporting hook has been forced to one side. It's bent. Why? To make room for the 'lever' to fit without impedance.'

'Why a stick?' Blair asked. 'It could have been the barrel of the B.S.A.'

'In the final stages it was. The shot was, I think, fired through the electrolier tube, itself wider than the rifle barrel. The very short length of tube left before the slug escaped would not interfere with the slug's line of flight. It was a continuation of the rifle barrel if you like.'

He sat considering for a second or two and then went on:

'First, though, our killer had to be sure of his aim. There just could not be any room for a mistake or the whole thing was doomed, and the potential killer with it. The killer had to fire blind because the electrolier tube was the only means he had of seeing his objective. Once the rifle was in place he couldn't see below. Our killer, I repeat, had to be certain. The only way to be that was to make trial shots until he got the right position.'

‘We don’t know that he did,’ Blair objected.

‘We do.’ Gossage pointed to the desk edge where the notches were visible in the polished wood. ‘Remember how I looked at these when we started to examine this study? I’m pretty sure now that they fit into place in the puzzle as the marks of test shots. Now, if we get in line with the center notch . . . ’

Gossage hauled himself out of the chair and went over to the desk, kneeled down so that he was looking at the vertical electrolier in almost a straight line.

‘If we do this,’ he explained, ‘we see that if the electrolier were tilted about a foot out of the perpendicular, a shot from it would strike the back of Darnworth’s head.’

Blair was nodding eagerly now: ‘So far, so good, sir.’

Gossage stood up again.

‘I imagine that the killer fired the first time purely by guesswork, but marked the floor upstairs with a pencil line to denote the angle at which he had the rifle tilted. Then, by trial and error, he finally got the right position and to that line he added a crosspiece to denote which line was the one he wanted. When the rifle was tilted to that position it must hit the same spot again below. He could make the test shots at his — or her — leisure. Once the shot had been fired the killer had only to let the electrolier resume its normal position, draw it up two links, and go away. That, I'm sure, is how it was done, and obviously it opens up a lot of possibilities.'

'I can name a few,' Blair said. 'It means that somebody knew Darnworth's habits to the last detail, knew that he never changed the position of the furniture in here.'

'Exactly, and this same somebody had ample time in which to prepare the scheme, for it must have taken many weeks to make the test shots, choose the right times for seeing the effect of the slugs before they were found, and so on. Thus we narrow the field. It's definitely somebody in the house that we're looking for and not an outsider. And we are also looking for somebody with a mighty ingenious mind.'

Then worry came and settled on Sergeant Blair like a cloud.

'We missed something, sir,' he said moodily. 'Something that kills the whole theory.'

'We have?' Gossage snatched his pipe from his teeth. 'Let's hear it . . . '

'When that electrolier moved a foot out of the perpendicular to aim at Darnworth the lights were still on, I take it?'

'Certainly they were. We have Craddock's assurance on that.'

'These twin lights would change the shadows in the room as they moved. Don't tell me Darnworth wouldn't notice the shadows shifting, because he would. Anybody would.'

Gossage returned his pipe to his mouth.

'Gosh, Harry, for a moment you had me really worried. I should have mentioned that I worked out that point. Darnworth wouldn't notice the shift in shadows — which I grant would take place — because his desk light was full on, another fact of which the killer was evidently aware. Look!'

Gossage sat in the swivel chair at the desk and a double shadow of his bead and shoulders was thrown on the blotter from the electrolier above and behind him. But when he switched on the desk light the white brilliance across the paper in front of him destroyed the shadows completely.

'Maybe it's time to check up on motives,' he decided. 'Let's see what we have. Louise? We know precious little about her. She had a chance to get the boxroom key. The wit to think out the plan? Never can tell with her sort. Crafty as a fox sometimes behind the cringing. Let's put her down as a 'possible' and leave it at that.'

Blair pulled out his notebook and wrote swiftly, then he sat and waited.

'Next,' Gossage went on, 'we have Preston, who also had the opportunity and, I don't doubt, the brains to think it all out. Excluding Mrs. Darnworth for the moment, I cannot see why, on some suitable occasion, he didn't get the boxroom key from Mrs. Darnworth's handbag and have a wax impression and then a key made from it. Since he has to be in the corridor every evening — and by his own admission, was certainly in it between 7 and 8 on the fatal evening — he looms as 'highly probable'. Motive? Very good one, I'd say. We know that he's fiercely loyal to Mrs. Darnworth, and from what we can gather, by Mrs. Darnworth's own admission amongst other things, she loathed and was loathed by her husband for the accident in which he involved her. An enemy of hers would therefore, I think, be an enemy of Preston's.'

'Do you believe that accident story is true, sir?' Blair asked. 'I mean, now you're sure she really isn't paralyzed.'

'I don't know, Harry, I just don't, but I'm pretty sure she didn't like her husband, or he her. Which brings us to the old girl herself. Did she do it?'

'I can't help but think so,' Blair said.

'I'm inclined to think,' said Gossage, 'that Mrs. Darnworth was really paralyzed by the accident to which she referred, but somehow she got better and never revealed the fact for reasons of her own. Anyway, let's put her down also as 'probable', though not 'highly'. These three — Louise, Preston, and Mrs. Darnworth — are all the strongest suspects because of their opportunity to have the key to the boxroom, but in each case there arises the question of what became of the rifle.

'As for the rest of them with their motives and alibis — we know that Crespin and Bride had a motive, and so perhaps in a lesser kind of way had Sheila and Elaine. With the exception of Bride's, the alibis are pretty sound. He was two hours and five minutes just waiting. Maybe right — maybe not. Elaine was out, too, of course, but the time wouldn't allow her to do much between leaving the vet's and getting back here. Crespin was asleep in bed, to which fact the butler testifies. And Sheila was playing the piano during the fatal time and there doesn't seem to be a pianola which could perhaps explain it. Or perhaps even a gramophone record . . . '

Gossage's voice trailed off as he

thought for a moment. Then: 'Well, let's put Crespin, Bride, Sheila and Elaine as 'remotely possible.' That brings us to Andrews. He, as butler, might have the opportunity to do the whole thing without much difficulty since he has the run of the house. Presumably he didn't like Darnworth. Put him as 'possible.' Now where does that get us?'

Blair considered his notebook and then summed up as though he were in court.

'Highly probable — Preston. Probable — Mrs. Darnworth. Possible — Louise and Andrews. Remotely possible — Crespin, Bride, Sheila and Elaine.'

Gossage said: 'I think for the moment that is as far as we can get — theoretically. Tomorrow I intend to hunt again for the weapon, and unless Mrs. Darnworth has something to say we'll investigate in the village. For the moment, let us go upstairs to see if the theory of the tilting electrolier is correct. We'll use my walking stick as a rifle barrel.'

Blair switched off the lights and locked the study door behind them, and Gossage picked up his stick from the hall wardrobe. In silence Blair and he ascended the stairs, got a flashlight and entered the boxroom.

Once the electrolier had been lowered three links Gossage drove his stick into the tube and forced it back easily enough, the balance perfect.

'Then there's no doubt about it, sir,' Blair said. 'That's how it was done. If only it were the end of the riddle instead of the beginning!'

14

Gossage retired at 10.30 and promptly went to sleep. Then he opened his eyes slowly and realized that the bed light had been switched on, that it was shining obliquely on to the anything but prepossessing face of Preston, bending over him. Nor was this all. Preston was gripping a penknife tightly in his right hand and the tip of the blade was pressed against Gossage's throat.

'Not a sound, Mr. Inspector, if y'know what's good for you,' Preston warned, his voice low. 'One move the wrong way and I'll cut your throat.'

Gossage lay motionless.

'What do you want?' he asked.

'To tell you a few things. I've had about all the hanky panky I mean to have from you, inspector. I've warned y'plenty of times about pesterin' the old lady with y'fool questions, and now I've run out of warnings. I know what's in y'mind.

inspector. You thinks to y'self — She can walk can the old lady. That means she probably murdered her husband and then said she couldn't walk just to make an alibi. But y'not going to do anything about it, Mr. Inspector, 'cause I'll slit' y'throat first. I won't have Mrs. Darnworth pestered no more. So I'm saying that — '

'Preston! Preston! What are you doing?'

The handyman stiffened. Slowly he straightened up and the knife was withdrawn from Gossage's throat. Gossage could see that Mrs. Darnworth was by the door, in a negligee. Standing on her own two feet.

'Preston, put that knife away!' she commanded.

'Yes, mum,' Preston muttered sullenly, and snapped it shut as he glared sideways at Gossage.

Mrs. Darnworth turned to the door and twisted the key in the lock. Then she came forward slowly, a smile of cold, bitter amusement on her face.

'You take too much for granted, Mr. Gossage,' she told him. 'You should lock your bedroom door. It's fortunate for you that I heard Preston prowling in the corridor. I opened my bedroom door just in time to see him entering your room. I rather expected it, so tonight I kept my room door key instead of letting Louise have it.'

'Thanks for walking in,' Gossage said, sitting erect in his vividly striped pyjama jacket. 'Preston, draw up a chair for Mrs. Darnworth.'

The handyman did so, ungracefully. Then he stood at the back or the chair as Mrs. Darnworth sat down.

'I observe,' Gossage remarked, 'that I was not mistaken in saying you can walk.'

'No, you were not mistaken . . . I had intended admitting the fact in the morning, but this incident has hurried it. I realize that it would be foolish of me to try to cross the law. It might also give rise to other entirely groundless suspicions. You could have found out the truth, anyway, and so it is better that the truth should come from me.'

Mrs. Darnworth turned her head to look at Preston.

‘And if I ever catch you playing about with that knife again, Preston, I’ll give you in charge,’ she snapped.

‘It was only to protect you, mum,’ he retorted.

‘Protect me? By committing murder? Man, where is your common sense? And that is what you intended, isn’t it?’

Preston said nothing.

‘Preston is under the impression — whether rightly or wrongly I do not know — that you think I murdered my husband and that I invented this paralysis story to create an alibi. The story I told you about the accident was the truth and my husband was responsible for it. Specialists who examined me all returned the same verdict — prognosis negative. I would never walk again. However, determination can do many things, Mr. Gossage. For three years I was paralyzed. Then gradually I began to discover that the use of my legs was returning. I consulted my own doctor in the village and he told me that a million-to-one chance had come off and that complete recovery was possible. For reasons of my own I forbade him to mention my prospects of recovery to anybody. Of the members of the household only Preston knew my secret. I knew I could trust him; he has been in my employ for 15 years. One other person, outside of the doctor and Preston, has known the facts all the time — Clinton Brown.'

Gossage nodded. 'You mentioned him at dinner last night and I mentioned him to you this evening. Honest, kind, and unambitious, I think you called him? I gather he lives in that cottage you visited?'

'Yes, he does,' Mrs. Darnworth admitted. Then she continued: 'Ambition, Mr. Gossage, has been my downfall. I was born in Bexley, and though I loved Clinton, he couldn't give me the money and position I wanted. Then Mr. Darnworth, at that time a fairly prosperous young financier, bought a house near Bexley. I married him, and 10 years ago we came here. Clinton never married. When things became too intolerable with my husband I used to seek solace with Clinton. When he heard of my accident he vowed he'd kill my husband and I had a struggle to dissuade him. I could only do it by letters because I was bedridden at that time . . . I really think it was because of him that I struggled back to health. But I took care that nobody in this house knew I had recovered.'

'What reason had you for concealing it?' Gossage asked.

Mrs. Darnworth smiled rather wistfully. 'I had the idea that by flinging my incapacitation in my husband's face day and night I'd bring about a sense of remorse — and I also thought I'd cause him to leave me everything when he died.'

'And he didn't leave anything to you? According to Miss Sheila?'

'No. He left everything to Sheila — on certain conditions, the exact details of which I don't yet know. I know these facts because my husband left a letter with the family solicitor, to be opened by me when my husband died. I have now had that letter. In it my husband says he doesn't intend to leave anything to his 'miserable wife' as he calls me, or his 'cowgirl' daughter, meaning Elaine. He says he is leaving everything to Sheila if she can live up to her reputation. The meaning of that escapes me. If she doesn't there are other dispositions that don't touch the family and cheat me out of my legal third as his widow. The will is to be proven tomorrow or Tuesday — or rather today since we are now in the early hours of Monday — and then we shall know the facts. The letter merely gives me advance warning not to expect anything . . .'

Mrs. Darnworth paused and then went on again.

'I tried desperately hard to swing them in my favor, Mr. Gossage. I even took sides with my husband against my own daughters in the belief that agreeing with his viewpoint would cause him to leave things to me at his demise. Ambition, you see — the crazy longing to have everything. I deserve to lose for my deception. It has not been easy for me to maintain a frigid, uncompromising attitude with my own children, and particularly Sheila, who is a highly talented girl.'

'I know it hasn't,' Gossage said, and the woman gave him a sharp look.

‘You know it hasn’t? How?’

‘I fathomed this alter ego of yours, Mrs. Darnworth, when my sergeant stumbled on certain things in the boxroom deed boxes. He acted without my authority, but of course I couldn’t help hearing the details of his findings. The hair of Sheila and Elaine in satin-lined boxes; Sheila’s first efforts with the alphabet; later, her manuscripts. Those are your treasures. They didn’t fit in with the general aspect of you deriding Sheila for everything she wrote.’

‘I played a cruel, bitter role for something I didn’t get.’ Mrs. Darnworth sighed, reflecting. ‘I don’t blame Sergeant Blair for finding those mementoes. I had the idea he might — or that you would. The manuscripts do belong to Sheila. Her father laughed them to scorn. I joined in to show that I agreed with his viewpoint. Sheila threw the manuscripts away, but I had Preston recover them and I read them for myself. At that time I was really disabled and had no safe place to keep them. I dare not let my husband know that I was in any way sympathetic toward either girl. I could not get up and down stairs, so I chose a sealed deed box in which to keep things, knowing my husband would never look there. In there I also kept the letters Clinton had written me many years ago.'

'Why did your husband so deride Sheila's efforts?'

'Because he hated girls and never gave them credit for being able to do anything intelligent. He wanted sons. That was another reason why he had no time for me . . . ' Jessica Darnworth pondered through an interval, then:

'However, to return to facts. I had the letter from the solicitors on the evening of the day you came, after they had been notified of my husband's death. I knew then that I had lost my battle, but the shock was not so very terrible because I had had advance warning of it by Sheila's remarks during dinner. I had to decide what I must do. I must let Clinton know. So yesterday afternoon I went to see him. I always have chosen Sunday because Bexley is so deserted on that day. In case anybody might see me, however, I always wear a veil to conceal my identity. I saw Clinton, Mr. Gossage, and . . . we are going to try and catch up on the wasted years. I fought a battle and lost it. I intend to make every fact known to my daughters and the household and then withdraw and leave Sheila to control matters as she sees best.'

'That, of course, is entirely up to you, madam,' Gossage said. 'I think you should know that in spite of everything your daughter has made good with her writing. She calls herself 'D. J. Harper'. Mr. Crespin told me in the strictest confidence.'

A slow smile spread over Mrs. Darnworth's face. 'That is wonderful news to me, Mr. Gossage — but by no means surprising. Sheila gets a lot of her determination from me, you know . . . D. J. Harper, eh? Good for Sheila — and thank you, Mr. Gossage.'

She rose to her feet with a certain air of quiet dignity.

'When the will has been read I shall make everything clear,' she said. 'And I'm glad you have been so understanding.'

'There's one thing more. Do you give your solemn word, Mrs. Darnworth, that you have not entered the boxroom recently — before your husband died?'

Something that looked like surprise crossed the woman's face.

'Of course I do, inspector. I haven't been in that room for years, when I last put Sheila's manuscript away.'

'Very well, madam. I believe you,' Gossage said. 'It makes things tougher for me, I'm afraid, but I still believe you. Tell me, did anybody besides you know that your husband was liable to drop dead from heart trouble?'

'Only Preston.' And Preston nodded slowly.

'As I understand it,' Mrs. Darnworth went on, 'you seemed to have some sort of theory about the study electrolier being connected with the death of my husband. Is that still your belief?'

'It is. I shouldn't tell you so, really, but I will. The electrolier definitely is connected with your husband's death, and somebody went in that boxroom before he died. Now you see why my suspicions swung toward you when I knew you could walk and also possessed the boxroom key.'

'Yes. I see.' She shrugged and looked genuinely mystified. 'I can only repeat what I've said. I've not been in that room for a long time.'

Gossages's eyes strayed to Preston.

'I haven't either,' he said, and his voice was, for him, surprisingly quiet. He added contritely: 'I'd like to say that I'm sorry for the way I carried on, Mr. Inspector, and I'd like to make it up to you.'

15

Mrs. Darnworth used her wheelchair at breakfast, but she cast a significant look towards Gossage as he took his place, Blair beside him.

'This morning,' she said, 'I want all of you to assemble in the lounge to hear the will read. Mr. Brakestone will be here at 10 o'clock for that purpose. Naturally, inspector — and you, Sergeant Blair — I do not include you.'

'Naturally,' Gossage conceded.

'Bit awkward for me,' Crespin said, rubbing his jaw reflectively. 'I'd planned to get down to the city immediately after breakfast. Work to be done, you know: for me the weekend is over.'

'I would much prefer you to stay,' Jessica Darnworth told him firmly. 'Not particularly because of the proving of the will, but because of a statement I shall make afterward. I shall also wish you to be present, Andrews,' she added, glancing at him. 'And the staff. I will ring for you when I require you to enter.'

'Very good, madam,' Andrews assented.

'I suppose I'm included, too?' Gregory Bride inquired.

'Certainly. I said 'all of you', did I not?'

'You gentlemen are assuming, I take it, that I have no objection to you going?' Gossage asked, glancing at them. 'I don't seem to remember that either of you asked my permission to leave.'

Both men looked surprised, and Barry Crespin put his mystification into words.

'But I understood that we were free to come and go as we chose. Or did I get the idea wrong?'

'You are free to come and go as long as you are staying at the manor here, because I do not wish to cause you any inconvenience — but I'd take it as a favor if you'd make arrangements to remain here until this matter of Mr. Darnworth's murder has been cleared up. I may wish to refer to one or other of you at any time upon some point of interest and I do not intend to have to chase either to Godalming or London after you.'

The two men looked at each other and then back at Gossage.

'Very well,' Crespin said. 'You're the boss, inspector. I'll ring up London and tell them to ring me back here if anything important turns up.'

'Thank you,' Gossage said, and looked at Bride. The scientist merely nodded; then he added: 'I can do my sort of work anywhere, if it comes to that. A piece of paper and my brains, plus a pencil, are all I need to work anything out.'

'After breakfast, Mr. Bride, there will be time for a short chat, I think, before you go into the lounge,' the inspector said. 'I've a point or two I'd like to clear up with you.'

'With pleasure,' Bride agreed.

Immediately the meal was over he gave a nod to Gregory Bride and they went to the music-room.

'Since the others will be assembling in the lounge and the study is closed for the time being, this is our quietest spot, Mr. Bride,' Gossage explained, as he closed the door. 'And don't look so bothered,' he added, smiling. 'Nothing serious, you know — just that old bugbear known as routine. It is your association with Mr. Darnworth that I wish to ask about. I understand that he financed several of your inventions?'

'That's right,' Bride agreed.

'What were these inventions? Any objections to telling me?'

'Not in the least: there's no secret about them. There were five inventions that Mr. Darnworth financed for me. A new type of can opener; a self-changing clockwork calendar; a new style of combination lock for safes; an electric bulb which burns continuously for several years without the filament breaking; and a magnetic device for motor cars to pick up tacks and steel filings before they get under the tires.'

'You managed to interest Mr. Darnworth in your inventions without the help of Miss Darnworth?'

'Elaine,' Bride said, 'never had anything to do with my interesting Darnworth in my inventions. I know that she said she became engaged to me so that she could 'press my wares' with the old man, so to speak — but that wasn't quite the truth.'

'I believe you came here this weekend for the purpose of interesting Mr. Darnworth in a new invention? Something so important that it necessitated your making a change of plan the moment you knew he had been murdered. What was this invention?'

'It's a new helicopter.'

'Can you describe it to me without becoming too technical?'

Bride nodded obligingly. 'Yes, I think so. This one-man helicopter I've designed has rotary propeller blades much narrower than the machine itself, which makes it capable of approaching closely to the side of a building or a ship. And it isn't anything like as noisy as the average helicopter.'

'Have you a working model of it?'

'In my laboratory workshop in Godalming I've a good full-sized job, ready to fly. All I have with me here are the blueprints, if you'd care to see them.'

Gossage smiled and shook his head. 'No thanks, Mr. Bride, I'll take your word for it. But why did you intend to apply to

Mr. Darnworth? Surely the air ministry is the proper opening for a helicopter?'

'Quite right, but getting the air ministry interested is no job for a chap like me. I've precious little influence and no business sense whatever. I was aiming to have Mr. Darnworth fix things up for me. We had a financial arrangement that was to have operated if the air ministry took up the idea. I didn't need ready cash finance this time as in other cases, since I have the test machine made. That is why, when Mr. Darnworth — er — died I went back home quickly and sent a letter to the air ministry to open preliminary discussions on my own account.'

'I see . . . Well, Mr. Bride, thanks for all you've told me. I shan't keep you any longer. Mrs. Darnworth will be expecting you in the lounge, I suppose.'

Bride left the music-room and Gossage remained there until Sergeant Blair came in.

'They're all gathered for the fray, sir,' he announced. 'Brakestone just arrived. That leaves us on our own — for a while, anyway.' He paused and raised a questioning eyebrow. 'Did you get anything out of Bride? I passed him in the hall.'

'Bride,' Gossage answered, 'is a fellow with dozens of bright ideas and his range of scientific invention seems to have no limit. His latest masterpiece — which brought him here this weekend and the development of which was cut short by Darnworth's death — is a one-man helicopter which can move and presumably become stationary beside a building. Added to that it is practically noiseless.'

'Helicopter!' Blair repeated. 'Why, it puts him right in line as having had the means of getting into and out of the boxroom. When he was missing for that two hours and five minutes he could perhaps have gone to his home in Godalming by bus, got into the helicopter, flown it here noiselessly in the dark, done the deed, and then brought the machine down in some deserted spot. Then he could have joined Elaine in the ordinary way. At the first reasonable opportunity — the following day no doubt — he probably flew the helicopter home again.'

Gossage said: 'I think the best thing we can do is go up to the boxroom and see if that window could be opened and shut from the outside. Then we'll have a last look for that rifle.'

'Won't be any good, sir, if Bride put it in the helicopter, as he probably did.'

'We'll look, just the same. Come on.'

As they reached the top of the stairs Gossage said: 'You've still got the key, Harry. Go ahead.'

Blair unlocked the boxroom door and they stepped inside and moved over to the window.

'As a matter of fact, sir,' Blair said, 'I had a good look at this yesterday while you were out on your ramble. There's no question but that it could be opened and shut from the outside, and here's how.'

He tugged out his penknife and snapped open the smallest blade.

'Being the sash variety, with a horizontal catch which simply pulls into the slot of the adjoining sash, makes it easier,' he went on. 'My blade, as you see, when I insert it from above goes easily between the two sashes You can see the point of it through the lower window glass. And gentle pressure snaps the catch back — so!'

The catch clicked back with hardly a sound.

'Pushing it from the top is equivalent to pushing it from below,' Blair added. 'The only difference is that from this side of the window it can't be pushed up from below because the glass is in the way.'

'How about closing the catch?'

'That's easy too. You fasten a double length of string round the center of the catch-bar — double length so you can withdraw it when finished — and have the two ends hanging down between the sashes. A very long piece of string, of course, so you can allow for raising the lower sash. You then close the window and jerk the string sharply and diagonally, holding both lengths at once. There is just enough central leverage to pull the catch forward, and this catch moves very easily. Snap she comes into position! Withdraw the string and off you go.'

'Yes, that's plain enough. Have you tried to prove your idea?'

'Only from the inside. I'd need a ladder to do it from the outside and I haven't tackled Preston about it. I thought you would perhaps do it: you can deal with him better than I can. Just the same, sir, I'm pretty sure it could be done.'

'Of course it could be done,' Gossage agreed. 'But what I want to know is how the killer did it without a ladder? The window sill is too narrow to balance upon, and it would require very steady positioning for a moment in order to pull the string at exactly the right angle. Otherwise the pull would be lost and the string might snap. That of itself, the sudden break, might conceivably precipitate the person concerned into the drive.'

'The helicopter, sir! I'm sure that's the answer.'

'Is it?' Gossage asked moodily. 'I can't imagine a helicopter being that steady. I could imagine some robot control gadget on the helicopter keeping it outside the window while Bride — if it was he — came inside this room. I can imagine him getting out again and into the helicopter, but I can't see him getting enough steadiness to pull the catch back in place. No, Harry, it doesn't fit in place properly. It isn't a neat job like the rest of the murder. There was some way by which the killer had perfect security on the narrow ledge.'

Blair flung the window up with a touch of exasperation.

'Not getting on very fast, sir, are we?' he asked bitterly. 'I'd forgotten the fact, too, that it would mean he could hardly get in and out of the window without leaving a trace of some kind, from shoes I mean. Yet look at this ledge and the woodwork. Not a sign of a shoe-scrape.'

16

Sergeant Blair completed his own part of the investigation and came back to the study to find Gossage already there, seated in the swivel chair by the desk, smoking complacently.

'Not a thing in the way of a weapon in the basement,' Blair reported.

'Same with me. I've looked in the unlikely places. Not a complete examination of everywhere because I trust Craddock. All I have done is go over the same ground again, but I ignored floorboards and behind cupboards and such like. I'm pretty sure that the rifle isn't in the house. And that being so, I'll hop to the next stepping-stone and have Morgan's Deep dragged. I'm pretty sure now we'll find the rifle there.'

He looked at two cellophane envelopes as Blair put them on the blotter.

'What are these, Harry?'

'I don't know, but it might be worth

sending to the forensic department for analysis, unless you want to have a shot at it yourself with your own stuff — '

'Not for me,' Gossage said firmly.

'I thought not, sir. Anyway, it's ash and clinkery stuff from the cellar grate, together with a few bits of hair — which may have come from the plaster somehow — and a few charred bits of a label. Here it is in this separate envelope. You can still see the number even though the stuff's been burned. Must have been gilt letters and figures originally, I'd say. Same as you can read the letters on the gold-lettered cigarette packet when you burn it.'

Gossage peered at the charred remains of the label carefully. Then he looked at the leaf of Blair's notebook on which he had written the serial number — CGF469.

'Good work, Harry. I think the best thing you can do is jump in the car and take the stuff back to the laboratory. Tell 'em to 'phone me the moment the analysis is complete.'

'I'll do that right away,' Blair agreed.

'There's just one other thing, too — about Crespin and Miss Sheila.'

'Oh? What about 'em?'

'They came down in the cellar while I was there. I kept out of sight. Sheila said something about 'it not mattering any more' and then she pulled a big yellow envelope from behind some loose bricks in the wall. I couldn't make out what it was. Then she and Crespin went back upstairs. They didn't know I watched them. I switched the light off when I heard their feet come along the hall towards the cellar steps.'

'All right, Harry, thanks,' Gossage said. 'I'll try to find out the significance behind the incident. Anything else?'

'No; that seems to cover everything for the moment.'

'Okay. Off you go to London with that stuff and be back as soon as you can.'

Blair picked up the envelope and left. His eyes narrowed in thought, Gossage refilled his pipe and lighted it. By the time he had ended this operation he seemed to have come to a decision. Pipe comfortably between his teeth, he departed from the study, locked it behind him, and strolled to the lounge. Only Mrs. Darnworth was present, gazing out absently on to the driveway. As Gossage entered she turned her head.

‘Hello, Mr. Gossage,’ she greeted quietly.

‘‘Nobody else about?’ he asked in surprise, glancing round.

‘Not at the moment. Elaine has gone to Mr. Findley’s and Mr. Bride has gone with her — part of the way, anyway. Sheila is in the summer house and Mr. Crespin is upstairs in his room, telephoning London on the extension to make arrangements for his indefinite absence.’

‘I see. I think I’ll pop over to the summer house later and have a word with Miss Sheila. There’s a small matter on my mind.’ Gossage paused and looked at the woman’s pale, set face thoughtfully. ‘I suppose they all know by this time?’

‘About my recovery?’ She smiled faintly. ‘Yes, they all know. The two men just took it in stony silence and regarded me with something of the contempt that, I suppose, I deserve. All Elaine said was that she presumed I knew my own business best, and after that she left me without another word. Sheila was the most generous. She seemed really glad that I've recovered, and generous child that she is, she wants me to stay on here as though nothing had ever happened. She's prepared to forgive the way I've behaved towards her.'

Gossage nodded slowly. 'And what are you going to do, Mrs. Darnworth?'

'As yet I don't quite know. I'm trying to make up my mind. As I had already been informed, the will leaves everything to Sheila. To Elaine and myself there are a few hundreds which, considering my husband's financial resources, may be classed more as a gesture of contempt than anything else.'

'Sheila,' Gossage said, 'is a remarkably generous type of girl, isn't she? The forgiving sort?'

'No doubt of it.'

'Has she always had such a happy temperament?'

'Always, yes. Only a girl with a spirit like she has could have risen above the veiled abuse of her father, her sister — and myself.'

'And how has she taken the fact that she inherits everything?'

'Quite calmly. In fact, she wants to share it between herself, Elaine, Mr. Crespin, and me. Since she'll be marrying him soon that is quite understandable, but he is against sharing, and I can't say I altogether blame him.'

'There's one point which I find a little puzzling, Mrs Darnworth,' Gossage said. 'As I see it, Mr. Darnworth had more contempt for Miss Sheila than for anybody else. He ridiculed her work, you say, and took every chance he could to make her embarrassed and uncomfortable. Yet he willed everything to her! That, to me, seems odd.'

Mrs. Darnworth turned to look at him, a thin smile on her lips.

'You don't know the conditions attendant on her inheritance, Mr. Gossage — the last grand gesture of scorn. It is a proviso that only became apparent when the will was read this morning. Before she can touch a penny Sheila must have published at least three novels — in a period of two years from the proving of the will, otherwise everything will be disposed of in other directions.'

'Well, Sheila has published more than three novels. I've read four Harper books myself.'

'Exactly, and that fact can be proved to Mr. Brakestone's satisfaction. Actually, the inheritance is Sheila's to use from now on because she can fulfill the demands of the will. But my husband was not aware — nor were any of us except Mr. Crespin — that Sheila had been accepted. She has admitted since that she kept it quiet for fear of further ridicule. Do you not see the cynical viciousness behind such a clause?'

'I believe I do,' Gossage admitted. 'Your husband did not really want any of you to have it, so he left it to the one whom he considered the least likely to conform to the conditions — the daughter whom he considered had no literary ability whatever. I gather he expected her to give up the fight or else work herself to bits to fulfill the clause.

But she has the laugh on him, because she achieved success without him knowing it!'

'Just that,' Mrs. Darnworth assented. 'When he felt generous enough to reveal that he was leaving everything to her he merely mentioned a proviso, but of course did not say what it was in case it gave her the chance to fight hard for success. As I've told you repeatedly, Mr. Gossage, my husband was a hard, ruthless, cynical man. Only he could have thought of such a thing.'

Gossage grinned admiringly. 'Good for Sheila! I think I'll go and have a word with her. See you again.'

When he neared the brick summer house he knocked the ashes out of his pipe and put it in his pocket, finally gained the door of the small but neat building and rapped.

From within the clicking of a typewriter ceased, then Sheila opened the door. Her mouth broke into a smile.

'Oh, Mr. Gossage! Want to see me?'

'If you don't mind? Just a word — '

'By all means. Come in.'

Gossage followed her slender figure into a one-room building, lighted by two big windows on either wall, with a table in the center of the mat-adorned floor. On the top of the table was a litter of papers and at one edge of it a typewriter. In one corner a feminine angle peeped out in the shape of a bowl of artificial flowers. On the rough walls were paintings and drawings, and beside the door an oil stove glowed.

'Nice place you have,' Gossage commented, settling in one of the tube-type chairs as the girl motioned to it.

'I like it,' she said. 'It's quiet, anyway.'

Gossage's eyes moved to the sketches and paintings and her sleepy gray eyes followed the action.

'They're mine,' she explained. 'Don't think too harshly of them, will you?'

'Hardly! I was just thinking that they're darned good. So you write books and get them published, play the piano brilliantly, and now I discover you paint and draw really well. You have many enviable talents, Miss Darnworth.'

'I feel sure you didn't drop in here just

to tell me that, Mr. Gossage.'

'No, Miss Darnworth. I had a much more definite reason. I'd like to know what you took from behind the wall of the basement this morning.'

'What I took from . . .' She stopped, her gray eyes wide open. 'Great Caesar, how do you know?' she gasped.

'I do, and that's all I can tell you. What's the explanation?'

'Oh, there's no mystery about it. Here it is.' Reaching out her hand to the center of the table she picked up a big envelope and from it tipped a wad of manuscript.

'A story?' Gossage questioned.

'Yes — rejected! My own fault, really: I made it too short. Can't think how I miscalculated. Anyway, back it came to roost about a week ago. The only big rejection I've had recently, and I didn't dare let my father know, or mother either, as circumstances were then. I managed to intercept it before it got to the house. I can see the postman come up the drive from here, you see.'

'Then you hid it?'

'In the only place I could feel was safe

until I had the time to lengthen it. Barry has promised to help me stretch the technical part. He hasn't even seen this one. I tried it out all on my own. I suppose I had the technical details too cramped somewhere. Anyway, there is no sinister secret about it as you can see.'

'Of course not,' Gossage chuckled. 'I was merely checking up. What's it about — this story of yours?'

'A murder. Just another of my mechanical crime mysteries. You wouldn't be interested, though. You know all about crime, whereas I cull most of my facts from textbooks and films.'

'Why not try me? Perhaps I can help. If I turn in some useful information you can lengthen the book and then dedicate it to 'The Crimson Rambler'.'

'Well, all right . . . ' The girl laughed, then turned her gaze towards the ceiling as she gathered together the threads of the plot. 'It's about a man who gets murdered in a room where there isn't a window and the door is bolted on the inside. He gets a bullet through his heart. Actually, though, the murderer fired the shot through the electrolier tube in the ceiling, which happened to be right above the dead man . . . No, that's a bit wrong. It was a bit in front of him, so it could aim at his heart. All the killer had to do was make experiments as to position and then shoot to kill . . . And there it is.'

17

Gossage sat motionless, staring at the girl. Her eyes had lowered now from their scrutiny of the ceiling and she was smiling in a way that was vaguely wistful. As the chief inspector still studied her in blank astonishment she wrinkled her overlong nose and sighed.

'Not too good, is it?'

'Oh, I don't know. It's possible, of course. In fact I'd say it's watertight for a sealed room problem. I take it, then, that the murderer did this from the room above?'

'That's right. He has his bedroom up there.'

Gossage said: 'Miss Darnworth, have you shown this manuscript to anybody?'

'Oh, no!' She raised a hand in momentary consternation. 'Only the publishers have seen it. Don't I keep saying I'm keeping it a secret because it was rejected?'

'Mr. Crespin hasn't helped you on it at all?'

'The manuscript? No. Maybe I've tossed out an idea or two concerning it, but otherwise he hasn't seen it. It's my own idea entirely, but since there is something wrong with it — even apart from the length — I'll have to call in help.'

Gossage nodded slowly, then with a smile he got to his feet.

'I'm simply taking up your time sitting here yarning, Miss Darnworth — and you've doubtless got, a lot to do. I know I have. I'll be on my way.'

He turned to look at her frankly.

'Get a shock when you learned the truth about your mother?'

'Let's just say — a surprise,' she countered. 'I'm glad it's all cleared up, though. It'll make life a good deal easier.'

'See you later,' he said, and began to stroll back toward the house.

All the time he walked he kept hearing Sheila's words over and over again, every detail of the story she had outlined. Of course the conditions were almost identical with those in which her father had been murdered. Yet she did not know — or apparently did not — how her father had been murdered. It seemed, though, that the two methods could hardly be coincidence.

Gossage spent a busy and profitable afternoon in company with Inspector Hoyle of the local force and Divisional Inspector Craddock. The afternoon's work yielded an air-rifle, B.S.A., dredged up from Morgan's Deep, which Gossage had promptly dispatched to Scotland Yard's forensic ballistics department by Blair the moment he had come back from London.

There were other things Gossage had seen, and was thinking about deeply. Footprints — definitely those of Elaine and Bride from where he had seen them standing beside Morgan's Deep — and curious gouged markings on the branch of a tree crooked like an elbow and overhanging the pond. There was something about those markings . . . Something —

He was still brooding about it when

Blair returned to the manor. As usual he and the chief inspector sought the latter's bedroom for privacy.

'Colonel Fordyce made his examination while I waited,' Blair said. 'There's no doubt about it. That rifle fired the slug that killed Darnworth. Specimen shots show an exact striker pin match.'

Gossage said: 'Suppose you wanted to get as high as the roof without ladders. What would you do?'

'Why,' said Blair, 'I'd try and shin up one of the gutter pipes, if it would hold me — if I couldn't use a ladder.'

'Any of the three pipes would hold you, Harry. I've had a look at them. Solid jobs, and square, too, which maker them easier to climb.'

'Are you suggesting that somebody climbed on to the roof?'

'I am. In fact the more I think of it, the more certain I become. After dinner tonight we're going to have Preston lend us one of the ladders and we're going up on the roof for a look around.'

Blair considered. 'If somebody did get up to the roof without leaving a trace, what happened then? How did they get in the boxroom?'

'Presumably by a rope, and the only place to fasten that would be round the chimney.'

'And the only two people outside who might be accountable for such happenings are Elaine Darnworth and Bride,' Blair said. 'So that is the lay of the land, is it? And they were near Morgan's Deep for no apparent reason except geological. I could think up a better alibi myself.'

'I'll remember that when you commit a murder,' Gossage chuckled getting to his feet. 'Unless, of course, I happen to be the victim . . . Well, I suppose we'd better start cleaning up for dinner —'

Gossage paused, an astonished look on his red face.

'Anything wrong?' Blair asked in surprise.

'I don't know whether to call it wrong or not,' Gossage said. 'It's just that I suddenly remembered Elaine telling me that she is an underwater swimmer, a golf player, a tennis player, and a gymnast.'

After dinner Gossage found Preston

and told him: 'I want to borrow a ladder. I'm going up on the roof.'

The handyman nodded promptly, feeling for his keys.

'And so y'shall, sir. In fact, I'll put the ladder up for you. Mighty heavy.'

'Thanks,' Gossage said. 'Which reminds me — Harry, buzz upstairs and get your flashlight. We're going to need it.'

Blair nodded and hurried off. When he reached the outdoors again in the still, mild night he found Preston in the act of heaving an extended ladder into position against the end of the front of the manor, Gossage standing close by watching him.

'Right up to the gutter, Preston, so we can get on the roof.'

'Y'not going to enjoy it much up there, sir,' Preston told him, his form faintly visible in the starlight. 'And it's a risky job in the dark. The roof's on a pretty steep slope.'

'I know, but I'll risk it. I've got soles on these golf shoes of mine. How about your shoes, Harry?'

Blair flashed on the torch and the beam fell upon the pair of goloshes he had donned, evidently when upstairs.

'You think of everything,' Gossage murmured, then after sundry heavings the ladder was in place and he said to Preston: 'Better stay at the bottom and stand guard — just in case anybody should come out of the house and blunder into it. We shan't be long.'

They reached the roof, and started to climb the slates. They were breathing hard when they gained the chimney-breast, clinging to it as though they had met a long lost friend.

Then they both sat astride the apex of the roof and looked about them.

Gossage turned the flashlight on the chimneybreast. A low murmur of satisfaction escaped him.

'Rustic brick, Harry. That's just the stuff we want! Nothing like it for shearing fibers from a rope — granting that one has ever been used up here.'

Gossage became silent, busily searching — and Blair, too. They examined every scrap of the brickwork where the beam touched, working their way round, but it was not until they were at the back of the chimney that Gossage found the traces he sought, low down, at the base of the stack.

'Hairs galore, and unless I'm crazy they're rope fibers,' he muttered, pointing to traces of them adhering to the rough brickwork. 'This is all I need.'

He pulled a cellophane envelope from his pocket, put several of the hairs into it.

'Analysis can establish whether or not they are rope fibers. If that should be so we start looking for something to match 'em. Anyway, let's get down.'

Gossage reached the ladder first and directed the beam of the flashlight along the slates for Blair's guidance.

The sergeant had just grasped the top of the ladder when Gossage muttered something. In swinging the torch beam round it had flashed across the gutter and he turned the beam back on the gutter.

'What's the trouble, sir?'

'I don't know whether it's trouble or luck,' the inspector answered. 'Won't take me long to find out, though. Let's get down.'

He continued the descent to the

ground and when Blair had dropped beside him he turned to Preston.

'Move this ladder a bit further along, Preston, will you? To about eight feet from the boxroom window.'

When finally the ladder was in position again Gossage climbed it by himself and from below Blair and Preston could see the flashlight wavering and sweeping as he examined the pipe carefully.

Presently he descended.

'Now move it to the same position on the other side of the front door,' he instructed. 'I mean about eight feet away from the left end of the house front, near Sergeant Blair's bedroom window.'

18

Again Preston obeyed, and again Gossage climbed.

When he came down he said: 'That'll be all,' and Preston took the ladder away.

'What's all this about, sir?' Blair asked.

'I don't know yet for sure — but it may be the answer I've been looking for. Let's see now . . . '

Feeling in his pocket Gossage brought out a rule and began to measure carefully along the base of the wall. He started about 10 feet from the left of the façade and finished up approximately the same distance from the opposite end. In silence Blair looked on, holding the torch beam steady. At the end of the performance Gossage closed the rule and stood thinking.

'Very interesting,' he commented finally. 'For a distance of approximately nine feet the paint is scraped off the iron gutter.'

'Oh?' Blair could not help sounding vague.

'Make the chimney breast the apex of an isosceles triangle,' Gossage said slowly. 'Take the left side of the gutter scrape limit as the B point of the triangle, and make the right hand gutter scrape limit as the C point. The apex we will call A. The scraped portion of the gutter then becomes the base line of the triangle. And what do you get?'

'I'm not sure, sir, but I'd suggest a straitjacket.'

'Harry, I am not trying to be funny!' Gossage said. 'That, expressed geometrically, is the answer to the boxroom riddle. And I'm not trying to imitate our friend Bride with his fourth dimension, either. Hold that torch steady for a moment.'

Blair did so, and flashed it on Gossage's scratchpad as he pulled it from his pocket. He turned the leaves until he came to the one upon which he had drawn the design of the front of the manor. Now he drew a slanting line from the chimneybreast to a point on the gutter over the third upper window from the left. The second line he drew from the chimney breast to the gutter at a point over the boxroom window.

'There!' he said. 'A triangle, with the scraped part of the gutter as the base line. Within that base line all the paint has been rubbed away. It's a true triangle in itself, even though it does not make a true triangle to scale with the house. To do that it would stretch from side to side. As it is, though, it's the answer to everything. I suppose you don't see what I'm driving at? You don't see that there is the explanation of how the killer got in and out of the boxroom?'

'By means of a triangle? I'll be hanged if I do. There's one thing I can see, sir — whoever figured out a geometrical murder must be a first-class mathematician. That seems to fit Gregory Bride. But I don't think he'd be thorough enough to climb a drainpipe and put a rope round the chimney. In that case I'd say Elaine had something to do with it. She told you that she is a gymnast. Then — '

Sergeant Blair stopped dead. Gossage could not see his expression, but he did hear a sharp intake of breath.

'Anything wrong, Harry?' he asked.

Blair whispered: 'No, sir, not at all.'

At that moment he couldn't say any more. It had dawned on him suddenly, and with perfect clearness, just how the killer had entered and left the boxroom. And he felt very much like kicking himself that he hadn't thought of it before. But the killer's identity remained as obscure as ever.

* * *

'Are you there, Inspector Gossage?'

The inquiry came floating out of the darkness to the accompaniment of feet crunching on the gravel. The tall, stooped figure of Andrews loomed up suddenly.

'I'm here,' the chief inspector responded. 'Does somebody want me?'

'On the telephone, sir. Scotland Yard.'

Gossage headed toward the front door leaving Blair and Andrews to follow. He had the telephone to his ear and was listening intently to the report from the forensic department as he watched

Andrews and Blair enter.

'Okay, I understand exactly,' he said finally. 'Thanks Arthur — just what I wanted. I'll be sending some fibers for analysis. Let me know what they are and keep them on file in readiness for a checkup when the time comes. Yes, I'll get the hair you want. 'By.'

He put the telephone back on its cradle and returned the pipe to his mouth. With a jerk of his head he had Blair follow him up to his bedroom. Blair waited until his chief had settled in the armchair, then as usual he perched on the edge of the bed.

Gossage said: 'It was Arthur with the results of the ash you found. It comprises wax, rubber burned into solution form, charred paper — that piece you found with the serial number on it — and quite a scattering of human hairs.'

'Human hairs?' Blair repeated sharply. 'But I thought they had come from plaster? Cow hairs.'

Gossage shook his head. 'The hairs are human and blond. And they are the hairs of a man.'

'There are only two men with blond

hair, sir — Crespin and Bride.'

'Exactly. Anyway, Arthur's mounted some specimens of the hairs and wants samples for checking purposes. We'll have to watch our chance to get some combings.'

'We ought to be able to do that easily enough, sir — but what puzzles me is what are hairs doing in the ashes of the cellar grate? You don't think a bit further in regard to that triangle that something — horrible has been going on, do you? Something like a dismemberment?'

'I certainly don't, and if you'll think you'll see why I don't.'

Blair frowned and made a troubled movement. 'If you don't mind I'll concentrate on that later on. I'd like to sort out the other details first. Wax and rubber solution, eh?'

'Originally rubber, I presume,' Gossage answered. 'Heat changed it that sticky half cindery mass which you found.'

'For the life of me I can't see where it fits in! In fact, rubber doesn't enter into the case at all, does it?'

'Rubber fits it all right, and so does

wax. Have a good think to yourself and see if I'm not right. Anyway . . . '

Gossage pulled out his scratchpad again and consulted it.

''C.G.F., four six nine',' he murmured. 'Hmmm — the number on the charred paper. All right: I think I know where to start tracing that back to its source, and tomorrow that's what I will do. In the meantime our job is to get some hair combings from the rooms of Crespin and Bride. Just hop down and see if everybody is in the lounge, will you?'

Blair nodded and went from the room quickly. When he came back he said:

'Coast's clear, sir. All of them are down there — Sheila writing, Crespin reading, the old girl reading, too, and Elaine and Bride are — '

'Don't tell me!' Gossage raised a hand. 'Arguing about the fourth dimension!'

Blair nodded and grinned. Gossage joined him at the doorway.

The inspector said: 'You take Bride's and I'll take Crespin's.'

Both doors were unlocked. Gossage glided into Crespin's room and went over to the dressing table. It only took him a couple of seconds to pass the comb through the hairbrush and collect the result. Then he returned silently to the corridor as Blair reappeared.

Each set of hairs Gossage put into a cellophane envelope, slipping a note in each to identify them; then he handed them to Blair with the rope fibers.

'Tomorrow, Harry, take this lot to Arthur at the Yard and get a comparison test on the hairs while you wait. They won't be perfect comparisons since it takes time to mount a hair, but it'll be near enough for our purpose. While you are doing that I'll be on my way to trace the catalogue number. Before either of us leaves tomorrow morning, though, we have another job to do — measure the exact distance from the manor to Morgan's Deep.'

Blair looked puzzled. 'But Bride told us that, sir. It's a quarter of a mile.'

'Nevertheless I prefer to be sure. Well, having got this far, we can go no farther, not until daylight. Best thing we can do is return downstairs and look amiable while we give away nothing.'

It was after breakfast the following morning before the chief inspector made any further reference to the case he was handling. Then, when the meal was over, he said pensively: 'How far is it from here to Morgan's Deep? Quarter of a mile?'

'That's right,' Bride nodded. 'In a straight line.'

'I've an idea I'd like to make sure of that, but the trouble is I've nothing long enough by which to measure. Unless any of you can help me?'

All save Elaine looked thoughtful. She got to her feet.

'If you'll all excuse me I think I'll be going to Mr. Findley's,' she announced curtly. 'I'm getting sick and tired of these experiments on your part, Mr. Gossage. In fact, they're becoming very silly!'

She stalked from the room, dressed in her usual riding breeches, shirt and jacket.

'Afraid there's nothing I can offer,' Crespin said. 'That is, not here. I've lots of stuff in my radio stores that would do — but that isn't much use, is it?'

'As for me — ' Bride started to say; then Sheila interrupted him.

'I believe I've got the very thing! A small drum of very fine wire. There's about half a mile of it. I think it would suit you fine, Inspector.'

Gossage nodded and got to his feet. 'Good. Let's see it.'

The girl hurried from the room and Gossage strolled out into the hall, Blair by his side. Behind them, Crespin and Bride stood waiting in obvious interest to see what was brewing.

Then Sheila came hurrying down the staircase. In one hand she was carrying a fair-sized cardboard drum, round the center of which was wound gleaming enameled copper wire.

Gossage raised an eyebrow in some surprise. 'It'll do fine. In fact, almost too good for the purpose. Anyway I shan't damage it, I hope. Harry, take it up to my room and fasten the end of the wire to the window, then drop the drum down to me.'

Blair nodded and hurried with the drum up the stairs. Gossage went outside.

Crespin, Bride and Sheila followed him as far as the front doorway and stopped there, watching proceedings. It was not long before Blair's head poked out of Gossage's bedroom window and the drum came whizzing down for the chief inspector to catch in his arms, a glinting wire trailing back to the window above.

Gossage started walking, playing out the wire as he went down the drive. The further he went, keeping well clear of trees, the heavier the wire sagged behind him . . . So out into Manor Larne and along it to the position of Morgan's Deep. Here, at last, by the old tree, he stopped, approximately half of the wire used up.

Carefully, the wire stretching back in a clear uninterrupted copper streak toward the manor, Gossage placed it over the notch on the inside of the branch shaped like a crooked elbow. He smiled to himself, particularly when he saw now that the enamel on the wire was badly scraped.

Allowing for rubbing on either side, the wire fitted the notch perfectly.

Removing it from over the tree branch

he went about the harder task of rewinding the wire as he returned to the lane, along the drive, and so back to the house. The trio was still in the front doorway, watching, and Blair was leaning out of the window.

'Okay, sir?' he called.

'Yes, Harry, okay. Unfasten the end and come on down.'

19

Almost immediately the writhing end of the wire came flying down in a coil and Gossage wound it on the drum, then he caught Sheila's eye and motioned her toward him. She said something to the two men and came across.

'Just what I wanted, Miss Sheila, and thanks very much,' Gossage said, handing it back to her. 'You'll find it's badly scraped, but it's remarkably good wire. Where did you get it?'

'Get it? Oh, Barry gave it to me months ago from his stock. He said there was about half a mile of wire on it. Surplus or something that he couldn't use. I remember he said something about it perhaps being useful for one or other of my 'realism' experiments — or, apart from that, it might come in handy for an on-the-spot radio repair if one were needed.'

'And did such an occasion arise?'

The girl shook her blonde head. 'No. I've kept it in a cupboard in my room from then until this morning.'

Gossage nodded and went down the drive. The two men in the front doorway returned into the hall.

'Well, sir?' Blair asked.

'At least,' the inspector said, we know at last how the rifle was removed from the house immediately after the murder.'

'We do? I'm afraid I don't get it. Something to do with the wire, you mean?'

'The killer made a continuous wire, double length, an endless belt, if you will. He looped it round the tree branch and carted it back to the house at an upper window. All he had to do was thread the lower wire through the trigger-guard on the rifle and secure it there, maybe with a bit of string. Or he could have put the wire once round the trigger guard and secured it that way. In fact, he probably did, otherwise we'd have found string still on the trigger guard.

'Then, the rifle hanging on the lower wire, he pulled the upper wire towards him. Automatically the under wire went away from the house and took the gun with it. It was kept going until it hit up against an obstacle — the tree branch. It being dark, this was the killer's only guide. Then? Snap the wire and the rifle fell in the pond. After that roll both lengths of wire back on the drum and join to the break with an over-and-over knot. The lower position of Morgan's Deep as compared to the manor would of course facilitate matters.'

'Very neat,' Blair said. 'And you are sure that that is the wire that did it?'

'No doubt of it. I didn't unravel it far enough to find a join, but the length and scratched enamelling is quite enough for me,' Gossage said. 'Definitely the wire was used from one of the upper windows facing the drive and Morgan's Deep and that means the windows of Crespin, Bride, and Mrs. Darnworth. At the time this wire was pulled Sheila was playing the piano, nor had she been out since dusk had fallen.'

'You mean to fix the wire in readiness?'

'Obviously it had to be fixed and

carried to the room in question — the window thereof, I mean. And somebody went to the pond and eliminated footprints, remember? There's our proof in that direction.'

'Crespin went out before his snooze,' Blair mused. 'And Bride went out, too, for over two hours. In other words, he was outside long enough and cannot say explicitly what he was up to. Sheila couldn't play the piano and fix and move the wire simultaneously. On the other hand, if her piano playing story is really a pack of lies, she could have gone out and fixed the wires and then, knowing Bride was out, could have gone to his room and got rid of the gun from there after the murder.

'Understand, sir,' Blair went on solemnly, 'that I am only considering the disposal of the rifle. All the other problems — the murder, the roof climb, your precious triangle and so on are not included, though from the way I read that triangle Sheila could just as easily have committed the crime as any other. She certainly couldn't have done anything through her mother's room because the old girl and Louise were in there, nor through Crespin's room since he was having a sleep. That leaves . . . '

'Two rooms you haven't accounted for,' Gossage said. 'I mean yours and mine — guest rooms. We hadn't arrived at that time.'

'I'd thought of them, but the arm of the triangle doesn't reach that far.'

'Good man!' The chief inspector beamed on him in pride, then he refrained from saying any more as the signs of mental struggle appeared on the sergeant's face. Then at length a gleam came into Blair's eyes.

'I mentioned Sheila having perhaps told a pack of lies, sir,' he said. 'It was only a casual observation, but now I can see that I might have more there than I thought. Do you suppose that Sheila really didn't play the piano? In fact, that it wasn't the piano playing at all!'

'Eh?' Gossage asked blankly. 'But we have everybody's word for it — '

'Yes, I know — but there is also a portable gramophone in the house. You told me that there's one in Mr. Crespin's room, and, what is more significant, he has a repeater-catch on it, a gadget which will swing the sound box back to the start of the record. Now, suppose that Sheila — knowing in advance what she intended to do, of course — bought a piano solo record of a tune which she is known to play a good deal, and put it on Crespin's gramophone. He would probably never notice that it had gone when he went in his room for a snooze.'

'Maybe not,' Gossage agreed. 'Well? Go on.'

'She went in the music room, put on the record, and then went out by the window. During that time the record kept on playing, and you can't tell with these classical piano pieces where they start or finish. She went outside and did whatever she had to do. Fixed the wire, committed the murder, and rid herself of the rifle.'

'All on one winding of the gramophone, I take it?'

'One winding on a portable, if it's a double spring, will play 12 minutes. It wouldn't take her any longer to hop to the Deep and fix the wire, and perhaps not much longer to commit the murder, for all we know.'

'I see. Then what did she do?'

'She went in to dinner in the usual way and waited until Crespin came down, I'll wager she'd find an opportunity somehow to get the portable back into his bedroom, The wire she had already put somewhere safe until she could return it to her own room. Maybe she put it in the summer house.'

'Then why didn't she leave it there?' Gossage asked.

'Because she knew that if the house were searched it was better to have things exactly where they had always been.'

Gossage stood brooding, a faint smile tugging the corners of his mouth.

'You're not doing badly, Harry,' he said presently. 'Anything else?'

'Yes. Proof!' Sergeant Blair looked dramatic for a moment. 'She had to get rid of that record at all costs, and so what did she do? At the first opportunity she hurried in the cellar and burned it in the grate. The analysis says wax, and that could mean record. The label that didn't lose its serial number even after burning could have been from the record, one of those plum-labeled ones, which have gilt letters on them. That serial number is a free gift to us, sir. I'll wager that if we can track it down we'll find that the record is exactly the tune Sheila was playing during that hour . . . Or for most of the time, anyway.'

'For which exact purpose I'm going out this morning,' Gossage said. 'I intend to call on various gramophone companies, find out who issued the record — according to the label — and see what I can pick up. Like you, I too suspect a gramophone record. In the meantime we had better help ourselves a bit by finding out what Sheila was playing during the hour. I should think Preston ought to know since he seems to listen to everything she plays. Incidentally,' the chief inspector added, 'you don't explain the bits of rubber tubing and the hairs?'

'I can't,' Blair said moodily. 'They'll probably fit in when we have the gramophone record business sorted out.

Maybe they were added as false clues.'

Gossage nodded seriously though there was still a vaguely humorous twinkle behind his glasses. Then he led the way along the drive and back into the hall. It did not take long to summon Preston and when questioned as to what Sheila had played he did not hesitate for a moment.

'Yes, sir, it was Rachmaninoff's Piano Concerto Number Three in D Minor.' He smiled rather thinly. 'If there's one I do know, sir, it's that. Miss Sheila's always playin' it — and she plays it beautifully.'

Gossage nodded. 'All right, Preston. That's all, thanks.'

The handyman went off and Blair looked supremely satisfied.

'Just as I said, sir! One of those pieces which you can't distinguish as either beginning or ending — unless you've got an ear for that sort of thing.'

'Which Preston has,' Gossage observed.

'I know, but he was upstairs and couldn't have heard too plainly. Besides, why should he think it curious if Miss Sheila played it once or twice, or even three times? Lots of people do that if they like a piece.'

'I think,' Gossage said, 'you'd better get off to the Yard, Harry, and get some results. I'll be on my way to the gramophone companies.'

'But I'll be using the car, sir. You can't walk round all the gramophone companies, surely? Not even you!'

Gossage grinned. 'I've no intention of being that crazy. There are several cars scattered around this place that I can borrow — Crespin's, Bride's, or even the family bus. I'll be okay. Oh, that reminds me! I want some special information, too . . . '

20

He went into the study, drew notepaper and envelope to him and wrote a brief note, sealing it. For superscription he put: Sir Leonard Harding, Assistant Commissioner, Department C, Scotland Yard. This done, he returned to the hall and handed it to Blair as he stood waiting in hat and coat.

'See the old man gets this in a hurry, Harry,' he instructed. 'And ask him to ring me here the moment he has any information. Stress the importance of it.'

Blair went, and Gossage turned into the lounge. Mrs Darnworth, Louise, Crespin, and Bride were there. Mrs. Darnworth was writing a letter and Louise was sewing. The two men were smoking and looking through newspapers

Barry Crespin was the first to speak.

'Mr. Gossage, how long do you intend to keep me a virtual prisoner here?' His voice was angry for once. 'I'm losing both time and money, and that's no way to build up my business! The longer I'm absent the simpler it is for my competitors to get ahead of me. I want to get back on the job.'

'I can understand that,' Gossage sympathized. 'You're a go-ahead chap with the ambition to own a chain of radio stores. I'm sorry if things are so irksome but I can't help it. However, I hope to clear matters up pretty soon now and then we'll be able to turn round a bit.'

'Can I be certain of that?' Crespin asked.

'I think so. It's just a matter of fitting a few final details into place.'

Mrs. Darnworth stopped writing and Louise lowered the trifle she was sewing. Only Gregory Bride went on reading, then his forehead puckered as something evidently interested him.

'The sooner I'm allowed to skip out of here the better I'll like it, too!' he declared. 'There's a chap here who's got a fairly similar idea to my new helicopter. If I don't act fast he may beat me to it.'

Gossage did not comment. He asked a question:

'Would either of you gentlemen mind lending me your car? Sergeant Blair's taken mine and I've a trip to make.'

'Use mine if you want to,' Crespin said, still aggrieved at the thought of the business he was missing. 'I've precious little chance to get about in it myself.'

'Or take mine,' Bride offered. 'It's only a two-seater, not a whacking big thing like Barry's. I'm sure mine will be more in your line, inspector.'

'Thanks, Mr. Bride. I'll reimburse you for petrol when I've seen how much I've used. Oh, I shan't be in to lunch,' he added to Mrs. Darnworth, and she nodded a grave assent as he went from the room.

* * *

It was late in the evening when Gossage and Blair met again.

'Hello, sir,' Blair greeted, as he saw the chief inspector in the hall. 'Shall I put the car in or — '

'No. I may be hopping to London myself.'

Gossage led the way up to his bedroom, and went on talking when they were within it.

'I borrowed Bride's car and broke down outside the village. I had Crespin tow me in with his big bus. Bride had gone to meet Elaine as usual.'

Blair nodded rather wonderingly. He couldn't be quite sure whether there was a wicked twinkle behind the inspector's glasses or not.

'Suppose you tell me how you've got on? You gave that note to the A.C.?'

'I did — and he'll do as you ask. Report as soon as possible.'

Gossage nodded and opened the door of his bedroom.

'I gave the fibers to forensic to keep,' he said. 'Which they will, as well as analyzing them — but we've got bad luck in regard to those hair combings, sir. Neither the hair of Crespin nor Bride matches with the hair in the cellar grate.'

'Doesn't, eh?' Gossage did not sound particularly concerned.

‘And,’ Blair added. ‘I think I know why. They belong to Sheila. She’s a blonde and we never took any of her hair specimens.’

‘The hairs belonged to a man Harry. Remember? All the difference in the world. And forensic wouldn’t make a mistake over that . . . Y’know, part of your theory about Sheila has already come unstuck so I suggest you remove the eagle eye from the poor lass.’

‘Unstuck, sir?’

‘I mean that serial number on the record. It doesn’t apply to a piano concerto. In fact, the serial number beginning with ‘C.G.F.’ never is used for musical compositions. So I’m afraid the idea of a portable gramophone playing while Sheila ‘did something’ is out.’

‘Then what does it apply to?’

‘That I don’t know yet. The Excel Gramophone Co. were the ones who finally identified the label as in their list, but it will take some time to check it back as it’s something special and not often asked for. When they’ve got the details they’ll ring me here.’

Blair nodded slowly.

'I could see the one big flaw in the gramophone record theory the moment you trotted it out,' Gossage said. 'Preston, up in the corridor, heard the piano quite clearly. Now you can't compare the playing of a portable gramophone with piano when it comes to volume. A radio, yes, with a volume control, but not a portable gramophone. That ruled it out for me. The walls in this house are mighty thick. You may remember that the idea of a record was brought up when we examined the study? At that time I thought just as you've been thinking — then I discarded it. I have all the details I need now, and I think I know the motive. It is up to the A.C. to verify that point for me. There is also one last detail I want to clear up, and for that I think I'll pop over to the Yard myself after dinner this evening. Then tomorrow we should be able to go, tie the job up, and get off. Unless, of course, the inquest turns up tomorrow and delays us.'

At dinner the most troubled looking person at the table was Gregory Bride.

He sat musing for quite a time even after the meal had started, then at last he looked across at Gossage.

'Barry has been telling me of the trouble you had with my car, Mr. Gossage,' he said. 'And I don't understand it. That battery is a reconditioned one and has served me faithfully. I've had a look at it and there are certainly no buckled plates to account for a short. In fact, it is charging itself again gradually. The hydrometer shows a specific gravity reading of 1,150 which means it isn't quite flat. You're sure it cut right out?'

'Just went dead,' Gossage said, and went on with his meal. 'However,' he added presently, 'if you do find any particular damage don't forget to let me know and I'll pay for it. Don't see how you can, though, when I never did anything except drive like any sane motorist.'

Bride shook his head in puzzlement and relapsed into silence. Then with a shrug he commenced his meal.

'I have something to ask you, Mr. Gossage,' Mrs. Darnworth said. She seemed to have been hesitating over the words for some time — had even seemed glad that Bride had forestalled her — but now she uttered them.

'I want your permission to leave here.'

'And go where?' Gossage asked, regarding her.

'London.' She paused, then went on quietly: 'Mr. Brown and I are going to be married there shortly. I went to see him this afternoon and that is the arrangement we came to.'

Gossage reflected with eyebrow raised then he glanced across at a sudden outburst from Sheila.

'I've tried every argument I can think of, inspector,' she declared, 'to try to make mother stay here. But she won't! I've told her that I don't bear any malice for the way she behaved toward me, that I'm prepared to forget everything and let her remain as she's always done — but it's no use. She insists on going.'

'Yes, Sheila, I do,' Mrs. Darnworth said firmly. 'You will be marrying Barry and this manor is rightfully yours. I would not consent to stay in it when you and Barry have your own lives to make. Very shortly you will be marrying Gregory, Elaine, and you will be leaving here, too. That is as it should be. I intend to catch up on the years I've lost. Sheila, my dear, you are very generous — perhaps too generous for your own good sometimes — and I don't intend to take advantage of it.'

Sheila relaxed and gave a little sigh.

'Well, there it is, I suppose. Nothing more I can do about it.'

'When would you wish to go to London, Mrs. Darnworth?' Gossage asked.

'Tomorrow.'

'I think, mother, that you're jumping to conclusions pretty freely regarding Gregory and me,' Elaine said. 'I don't believe in quick marriages — and if it comes to that I'm by no means sure that I'll marry at all.'

'But — ' Gregory Bride opened his mouth, gasped, then swallowed hard. 'But it's all arranged!' he protested.

'From your point of view, maybe — but we are only engaged, Greg. You know the type of woman I am. I like my dogs, the open air, my horses. I might consider finally that marriage isn't worth having as far as I'm concerned. In any event I expect to remain at the manor for some time yet because I like it, and no sense of misguided duty towards Sheila is going to turn me out of it! You can't offer me a place anything like so beautiful, can you, Greg?'

'Well no — not yet,' he admitted despondently. 'But I shall in time, as my royalties grow bigger.'

'Then while you build up I'll remain here,' Elaine said. 'I'm sure dear, generous Sheila won't raise any objections?'

'That sort of decision is just typical of your rotten selfishness, Elly!' Sheila declared. 'You're not doing it because you don't want to marry Greg, or because you like horses and dogs: you're doing it because I happen to have inherited the manor and want to live here with Barry as my husband. You're out to upset it! How well I know you!'

'That's right, I am.' Elaine agreed calmly.

'When I become Sheila's husband I

may have something to say about staying here,' Crespin said grimly, hard lights on his eyes. 'There are ways of getting rid of people you don't want, you know.'

'As dad found out,' Elaine commented.

'It seems to me that most of you are developing your plans very thoroughly without regard to one thing — the reason for me being here,' Gossage said. 'I can't allow you to leave just yet, Mrs. Darnworth, nor can I permit any of you others to make any variation in your present activities. After tomorrow, though, I'm hoping you will be pretty free to do as you wish.''

'So you actually have hopes of bringing the case to an end?' Elaine asked cynically. 'Well, it's about time! And I suppose it is one of us in the house?'

Gossage looked round on the faces. He saw tenseness in every one of them — even in the face of Andrews as he hovered in attendance.

'Yes,' he acknowledged. 'And I'm going to give that person a chance to come into the open. I don't say it will mean any less severe sentence, but the law does incline favorably toward a complete confession of guilt. If that person does want to confess I'm willing to listen in private.'

He paused for a moment and then went on deliberately:

'After dinner I am driving to the Yard. I expect to be back here again some time before midnight when I shall go straight up to my room. I invite the killer to come to my room at midnight and confess. As for the rest of you, I rely on your decency not to watch my room. If the offer is not accepted, I shall bring every agency of the law to bear with all the evidence I have collected. Believe me, all of you, there is no longer any room for doubt.'

21

Gossage left the house at a quarter to 9 and Blair, to escape questions from the others in the house, went up to his room — and fell asleep. It was 12.10 when he woke, and filled with a sense of profound shame he hurried to Gossage's bedroom and knocked lightly on the door.

There was no responding voice or sign of movement. Blair frowned worriedly to himself and turned the door handle, peered into the dark beyond.

'You there, sir?' he asked softly, feeling for the light switch — but to his surprise it had no effect when he pressed it down.

Then Gossage's voice reached him.

'Come in, Harry. I'm in the chair near the bed. You needn't try to turn on the light; I've taken the bulbs out. Close the door but don't lock it.'

Puzzled, Blair obeyed the order and groped his way across the room until he could see a dim outline where Gossage was seated.

'What's the idea of sitting here in the dark, sir?'

'I'm waiting for the killer to pay me a visit.'

'Pay you a visit? Why should he?'

'Because it's inevitable,' Gossage answered. 'At dinner I made it perfectly clear that I know the killer's identity. I gave a chance of confession at midnight — which chance I was more or less sure would never be taken. If you knew yourself to be a murderer and were going to be arrested, would you hesitate at destroying the person who could expose you? Would you let that person sleep comfortably all night and then calmly wait to be arrested next day? With one murder done, why not another? Incidentally, I had Louise here at midnight — not to confess but to tell the name of the murderer. She knew she could get me alone at midnight, and apparently she's been trying to for long enough.'

'So Louise knows, does she,' Blair murmured. 'Y'know, I rather thought you were taking a lot for granted at dinner when you made that offer.'

'A certain person,' Gossage said, 'is going to try very hard to get rid of me before morning — probably in the small hours. That's why I'm seated here waiting. I don't intend to be nabbed. I was going to tackle it on my own account but I'm glad to have your help.'

'I'm afraid I fell asleep,' Blair muttered. 'How did you get on at the Yard?'

'Excellently. Not only did I get what I wanted from the forensic department but I also got the report I'd been waiting for from the A.C. I got back here about 11.30, and shortly after the manager of the Excel Gramophone Co. rang me up from his home with the information I wanted about that catalogue number.'

'Then who is the killer — ?'

'Hush!' Gossage cautioned. 'You hear something?'

After a moment or two the sergeant did — so slight that had he not been keyed to notice it, it would have escaped attention. It was the sound of feet moving gently in the corridor outside. After a while they stopped and there was a long pause.

Then very slowly the bedroom door began to open. It was only by the very faint creak it gave at the hinges that the fact was noticeable at all.

It was when there was the slight sound of the door closing that Gossage spoke sharply.

'Don't move from where you are. I have you covered.'

Blair waited wonderingly. As far as he knew the chief was not carrying a gun.

'I know just why you've come here,' Gossage proceeded, 'and it isn't to confess. It may be with the idea of strangling me or knifing me. I wondered what you would do — whether you would enter by the window or the door. Then it occurred to me you would probably try the easiest way first. That's why I left the door unlocked for you — though maybe you knew about that from Preston's activities a few nights ago. I never lock a door: I trust people — up to a point.'

In the darkness of the room, now his eyes were getting used to it, Blair could see a dim outline against the door

— but that was all.

'I suppose,' the visitor said, 'I've only myself to thank for you being in readiness for me. I should have known.'

'You should have,' Gossage agreed, 'but like many killers you did your best to overreach yourself.'

Blair identified the speaker by the voice, but he still couldn't see how . . .

Suddenly the visitor turned on a flashlight and the beam was blinding for a moment. Blair covered his eyes and Gossage looked away momentarily.

'I don't see any gun,' the voice behind the brilliance said. 'What sort of a trick are you trying to pull, inspector?'

'I didn't say I had a gun. I said I had you covered — and I have — '

Gossage's right arm, which had been dangling over the arm of the easy chair, whirled up suddenly and what seemed to be a glittering bar sailed through the air. It smashed the torch out of the visitor's hand and dashed the room in darkness again.

'My walking stick,' the chief inspector explained. 'Let me tell you why there are no lights on in here. I wanted you to come in unsuspecting. I'll have Blair put them on again in a moment — '

'Lucky for you Blair's here,' the visitor snapped. 'Otherwise I'd have only had you to deal with . . . I'm not idiot enough to take on both of you — not with only a knife, anyway.'

There was a click like the blade of a knife shutting.

'You don't think,' the voice asked, 'that I'd be idiot enough to admit anything, do you?'

''No — and I don't think you're an idiot, either. In fact, you are very clever. I know everything you did, and how you did it.'

Blair got up silently and went over to the small bedside table where he began to feel round for the bulbs. But silent though he was, the visitor evidently heard the movements and knew that attention was relaxed. He shifted suddenly in the dark, there was the sound of the door opening quickly — then he had fled.

'Quick!' Gossage yelled, and dived across the room.

Blair blundered after him, just in time to see the inspector in the glow at the end of the corridor, chasing a figure toward the staircase. Gossage dived from the top step on the back of his quarry. They both went rolling down the stairs to the bottom, dimly visible in the yellow light, which glowed over the front door.

At a sound Blair glanced behind him. A door had opened and Sheila was on view in the light streaming from her bedroom — her hair flowing and a robe drawn about her. Blair dashed down the stairs and with his strength added to Gossage's the struggle in the hall was brought to a swift end.

Panting, swearing under his breath, his hair disheveled, Barry Crespin scrambled to his feet.

Blair held Crespin while Gossage switched on all the lights. He glanced back to the staircase to see Sheila, Elaine and Mrs. Darnworth, while behind them loomed the startled Gregory Bride, and farther back still, like a ghost, Louise. Evidently the noise had aroused each one of them.

Crespin was taken into the lounge and almost flung into an armchair.

'Do I have to sit here and be stared at?' he demanded, flashing a glance at the others as they came in silently.

'If you are having publicity now you've only yourself to thank,' Gossage told him. 'If you had had the sense to come to my room at midnight and tell the truth I could have spared you all this.'

'What does all this mean, inspector?' Sheila asked, obviously utterly bewildered. 'You can't mean that — that Barry — '

'I'm sorry, Miss Sheila,' Gossage said. 'Facts speak for themselves . . . Barry Crespin,' he went on, turning back to him, 'I arrest you for the murder of Warner Darnworth . . . ' And he added the usual note of warning.

'You arrest me!' Crespin gave a sour smile and tossed the hair back from his face. 'You haven't an atom of proof that would ever hold in a court of law.'

Blair began writing steadily in his

notebook and Crespin took stock of the fact. He set his mouth harshly.

'I'm not saying anything,' he decided flatly.

Gossage nodded. 'All right. Sergeant, go with Mr. Crespin to his room and see that he packs his things. We are returning to London immediately.'

'Yes, sir.'

The moment they had gone, Gossage found himself surrounded by the other members of the party.

'What are the facts, inspector?' Sheila demanded helplessly. 'I can't believe that Barry would do such a thing.'

'If I were not sure of my ground, Miss Sheila, I would not have charged him with the murder,' Gossage answered briefly.

'No surprise to me,' Elaine commented. 'I didn't know it was he, mind you, until dinner tonight, when he said there were more ways of getting rid of people — or something like that.'

'Barry seemed such a decent chap, too,' Bride commented, looking almost foolishly astonished.

Andrews and Preston, hastily dressed, came into the room. The butler looked about him.

'Begging your pardon, but I heard sounds — '

'Preston,' Gossage interrupted, 'you might get my car out of the garage. I shall be leaving for London immediately.'

Preston nodded and went across the hall. Gossage turned to the group.

'I am not allowed to divulge any facts,' he said. 'I would like to, if only to have you realize, Miss Sheila, that you have been wasting your charm and talents on a man of Crespin's caliber. When you attend the court proceedings everything will become clear to you.'

He glanced towards the staircase. Crespin, in hat and overcoat and carrying a traveling case, was coming down. Over one shoulder was his golf bag.

'I shall not need that as an exhibit,' Gossage told him, looking at it.

Crespin looked at the group in the lounge doorway.

'Looks as if the party's over,' he said, shrugging. 'Sorry, Sheila — but anyway you'll get on better without that father of yours always pestering you. All right, inspector, I'm ready,' he added, and moved towards the front door.

22

Despite a sleepless night, Sergeant Blair was at the office in Whitehall early the following morning. He wanted to know the facts, not only out of sheer curiosity, but to check for himself how far wrong — or right — he was. To his irritation Gossage had not yet arrived, so he busied himself in setting out the various notes in the form of a dossier, and generally acting — as he always did when in the office — as the chief inspector's secretary.

At 10 o'clock Gossage presented himself — red-faced, genial, and looking supremely satisfied.

''Morning, Harry,' he greeted. 'Still decent weather. I'm planning a lot of work in the garden this weekend if I can get the time.'

'Yes, sir.' Blair couldn't keep things bottled up any longer. 'But about Crespin!'

'Crespin?' Gossage settled in the swivel

chair before his desk. 'Well, what about him? He's formally charged, locked up, and we have an inquest to attend later this morning. What more do you want?'

'If it's all the same to you, sir, an explanation. I'm afraid I don't know how you arrived at some of your conclusions.'

Gossage chuckled good naturedly and brought out his pipe. 'Well. I have a few minutes to spare, so perhaps I can set your mind at rest. Take a seat. It makes it easier that Crespin decided to confess. Much of his statement bears out my own conclusions. But this statement gives me proof. I take it that you have the idea of the triangle clear in your mind, Harry?'

'Well, sort of. I can see that since we found evidence of rope around the chimney — but not on the side facing the drive — it meant that a rope had been put round the chimney breast, doubled so that it would be easily withdrawn afterward. It was then taken over a point of the gutter over Crespin's window, and moved along the gutter until it was over the boxroom window. That rope movement abrased the paint from the gutter

— the base of the triangle. I can also see that that abrasion could not have been made by rope alone without it having a weight on it, So, somebody got from Crespin's room — Crespin himself I suppose — to the boxroom by swinging on the rope, after the fashion of the weight on a pendulum. When the murder had been committed the murderer swung back to the starting point and withdrew the rope.'

'Dead right,' Gossage approved. 'But why the doubts in your mind about Crespin, Harry? The fact that the rope ended at Crespin's window, third from the left, was surely sufficient clue that Crespin was our man? It was to me — though I had begun to suspect him before that.'

'I suspected it might be Crespin, sir,' Blair answered, 'but I couldn't reconcile it with him being asleep. I preferred to consider Elaine, who says she is a gymnast — not Crespin, who has no such qualification whatever.'

'He has a better one,' the chief inspector said.

'Better! I — I don't understand . . . '

'He told me — and I told you, when we were entering the study after I had rescued you from Bride's four-dimensional theories, that when war broke out he left Switzerland where he had been mountaineering. To a man who can mountaineer in Switzerland the job of swinging from one window to another would be child's play.'

Blair sighed and looked annoyed. 'I had completely forgotten that, sir. What, then, were his movements?'

'I'll tell you how I worked them out, and you can take it for granted that they're right because Crespin has verified them in his statement. He went out before that retirement to his bedroom. Before he went out he took from Sheila's bedroom that coil of wire. Her door was not locked, a fact of which he had made himself certain through often being in the house.

'He fastened one end of the wire to his bedroom window and tossed the drum into the drive; he also fastened a piece of string to haul up the drum upon his return. Then he fixed the wire in the way we already know, obviously eradicating his prints in the mud. When he came into the house from his 'stroll' he had also been up on the roof and thrown round the chimney breast a long, strong tow rope from his car, the ends of which were dangling over his bedroom window. Naturally he climbed one of the gutter pipes, once again a trifle to a man used to mountain-climbing. Clear so far?'

'Not entirely. How did he climb the pipe without leaving a mark?'

'He used crude goloshes made out of inner tubes of tires, which gave him a firm grip and left no tread print behind. When he had finished his roof activities he put the 'goloshes' in his pocket, entered the house, drew up the wire drum by the string he had already fastened to it, and there he was. Before going up to his bedroom to do this he had told Andrews he was going for a snooze and left his instructions for 7.30.'

'Inner tubes,' Blair repeated. 'Then that accounts for the burned rubber in the cellar grate?'

'It does, yes — but let me go on. Just prior to 7.30 he fastened the rope about him, using his makeshift goloshes again for a firm foot grip, and swung from window to window. He opened the window easily enough, having steady support from the rope. In any case, he had rehearsed the task several times in order to make his test shots with the rifle. And on the occasion of the murder he had the rifle with him, of course. The previous weekend, he now confesses, he lowered the electrolier three links, so the thing was all set. He put in the rifle, levered it to the T mark, and fired. He then pulled the electrolier up again to the normal link and left the way he had come, snapping the catch in place with string.

'So he returned to his bedroom — some little time after 7.30, and knowing Andrews would be punctual, he knew he had been in the bedroom in the interval and seen him asleep. Naturally he — Crespin — closed his bedroom window.'

Blair had started to speak, but Gossage checked him.

'I know what's bothering you. Harry, and I'll clear it up in a minute. Getting back into his room Crespin simply pulled one end of the rope, and being double it came down from the chimney breast. He put it out of sight somewhere, and at a guess — which he hasn't admitted — I'd say he wound it round his body where the police couldn't find it. At the first chance he returned it to his car. Being plump, the extra size of the rope, not too thick but very strong, would not be noticed. He rid himself of the gun by the method we worked out and returned the drum to Sheila's room when he saw Preston take Mrs. Darnworth downstairs. That was only the work of a moment — but Louise, who had stayed behind to do something for Mrs. Darnworth, saw him entering Sheila's room with the wire drum. She withdrew quickly, and not suspecting anything then, said nothing about it — until the wire reappeared yesterday morning: then last night she told me what she had seen.'

'All right, sir, but how was Crespin seen and heard asleep and yet doing all this at the same time?'

'The answer was in the ashes of the cellar grate. You suspected a piano record for the self-playing repeater gramophone. I did at first — then I thought of a different type of record. An effects record, such as those which are used for crowds clapping or people sneezing and things like that.'

'My hat,' Blair muttered. 'I'm beginning to get it!'

'In this case, as the catalogue number has proved, the record was of 'Man Snoring'. That gramophone was in the bed, the clothes supported away from the sound box and all the time Crespin was away it was giving repeated snores. At one winding, as you said, that gramophone runs for 12 minutes, and even more time could be gained by running the record at half speed. That would just have the effect of making the snores deeper. It lasted long enough for Crespin's purpose anyway. All he had to do was make a rough outline of his body in the bed, cover it up to the top of the head, and Andrews, seeing the hair and hearing the snores would not try to wake up the 'sleeper' when he had been told not to. And the bedclothes were so fixed that the 'face' was buried — '

'The hair, sir — '

'The hairs in the ash which nobody could identify as anybody's in the house were of course from a wig. Well, once his job was done, Crespin, I hazarded, would smash the record in bits and carry it in his pocket with the inner tube 'goloshes' and wig. At the first chance he burned them in the cellar grate, but bits remained to fit into the puzzle.'

'How did you get on the track of a gramophone record, sir?'

'Chiefly the fact that the gramophone was there at all. He had made it clear that radio was his vocation and avocation. Why, then, I asked myself, should there be such interest in a gramophone? He never played a record all the time we were there, so I thought maybe there was another reason for the gramophone.'

'That's clear enough,' Blair admitted. 'And of course he would know that the furniture in the study was never moved

— a prime factor if his scheme was to succeed — and, come to think of it, a radio engineer would be able to get the copper to make that false rosette in the electrolier.'

'Right,' Gossage agreed.

'You speak pretty confidently, sir, about him using his tow rope for the window-to-window act. How do you know?'

'Proof,' Gossage grinned. 'And I don't mean his confession either. I contrived a breakdown yesterday with Bride's car simply by using the starter until the battery went flat. I sent for Crespin — knowing that Bride would have gone to meet Elaine — and had him tow me in. While pretending to fool with the knot, I cut some fiber from it. In the forensic department they match exactly with those taken from the chimney.'

'That about seals it,' Blair admitted.

'But why didn't you use Crespin's car in the first place? Or didn't you have the chance?'

'Oh, yes, I had the chance. It occurred to me though that the tow rope would be locked in the back of the car — and, as I found when Crespin arrived, it was. I would have had to ask him for the key and that might have aroused his suspicions.'

Blair said: 'He did all that in the boxroom without noise, I take it?'

'Crespin thought that part out with ingenuity. He knew Sheila played the piano for an hour each evening, and he admitted to us that he had seen Preston on the landing many an evening listening to Sheila's playing. He relied on Preston being so busy listening to the strains from below that the few slight boxroom sounds would escape notice — that, and the thick door and walls. The guess was right.'

The chief inspector put his pipe on the desk and reflected.

'I think,' he said, 'I first settled my mind on Crespin when I heard that of all the people in the manor after the murder he was the only one who looked 'grim', to quote Craddock.'

'And the motive?'

'Money,' Gossage said. 'It peeped out in a dozen places, and it seemed at its most pointed when Mrs. Darnworth told me that Sheila's wish was to share the money between herself, Elaine, Crespin and her mother. Then there was Crespin's own declaration that he wanted a chain of radio stores. There were other pointers, too, which escape me now but which confirmed his one obsession — money and progress. Further revelation came when he revealed that only he knew Sheila would benefit from the will — apart from the girl herself knowing, of course. Then it was I began to see light. Ignoring the proviso he had evidently planned from that moment to get rid of the old man and, when Sheila inherited the money, use most of it for his own advancement. She was just the type to hand it over without a murmur.'

'Nice chap,' Blair commented sourly.

'He gave Sheila the copper wire months ahead when the plan first matured in his mind, and as good as told her where to put it against the time when he would need it. Then gradually, each weekend he says, he worked out the plan to perfection. His mending of the radio was quite genuine, to give an excuse for going to bed — but he had fixed the radio on his last visit so it would conk out.'

'How do you think he got the rifle in the house, sir?'

'Golf bag, I'd say. Cover it up nicely. To make sure of his motive I had the assistant commissioner check up on his business activities and it seems he was up to his ears in debt with his notions for chain stores. Sheila's money could have saved him.

'His plan wasn't so original, either,' Gossage added, getting to his feet. 'For that matter, Harry, crimes of a mechanical nature rarely are. As we know from records, most murders are planned on the lines of something gone before. They are imitative. In this case Sheila had the method in her novel. Though she said she had not allowed Crespin to see the manuscript, she did say that she had 'tossed out an idea or two' concerning it. I'll gamble he got his ideas from that. Unconsciously Sheila had modeled her plot round some familiar point in the manor and it suited Crespin's purpose to the ground.'

There was silence in the office overlooking the Embankment. Gossage strolled to the window, hands in pockets.

'That's that, Harry,' he said, shrugging. 'What the Darnworths will do now with Crespin out of the way, I don't know, and frankly I don't care. The worse part is behind us — bar inquest and trial. And ahead of me, I hope, is a weekend in the garden with its clean earth instead of the ruthless machinations of a murderer's mind.'

THE END

We do hope that you have enjoyed reading this large print book.

Did you know that all of our titles are available for purchase?

We publish a wide range of high quality large print books including:
Romances, Mysteries, Classics
General Fiction
Non Fiction and Westerns

Special interest titles available in large print are:
The Little Oxford Dictionary
Music Book, Song Book
Hymn Book, Service Book

Also available from us courtesy of Oxford University Press:
Young Readers' Dictionary
(large print edition)
Young Readers' Thesaurus
(large print edition)

For further information or a free brochure, please contact us at:
Ulverscroft Large Print Books Ltd.,
The Green, Bradgate Road, Anstey,
Leicester, LE7 7FU, England.
Tel: (00 44) **0116 236 4325**
Fax: (00 44) **0116 234 0205**